PUBLISHER'S NOTE

This is the ninth volume of Charlie Small's amazing journals an it literally fell out of the sky! I was rock-climbing in the Py ees, edging my way towards a large nest on a high an onely ledge, when I heard a raucous cry behind me. Loo ing out across the rocky valley, I saw a lammergeier cir g in the sky.

e bird dived from the heavens and, thinking it was goi to attack, I hurriedly scrambled away from its nest. But the bird swooped in low, something dropped from its ghty talons, landing with a painful thump in my lap. Ima e my surprise when I saw it was a brand new Charlie Sma ournal! Packed full of Charlie's fantastic drawings, it tells e tale of what is probably his most cosmic adventure so fa I put it in my rucksack and, as soon as I reached base cam I sent it off to the publisher by pack mule.

T re must be other notebooks to find, so please keep your yes peeled. If you do come across an amazing diary, or se an eight-year-old boy wearing a battered rucksack, pleas et me know at the website:

www.charliesmall.co.uk

(Ni elodious Trumpery Ward, Custodian of the Charlie Small Journals)

CHARLIE SMALL JOURNAL 9: PLANET OF THE GERKS
A RED FOX BOOK 978 1 782 95329 6

First published in Great Britain by David Fickling Books,
previously an imprint of Random House Children's Publishers UK
A Penguin Random House Company

Penguin
Random House
UK

This Red Fox edition published 2015

1 3 5 7 9 10 8 6 4 2

MIX
Paper from
responsible sources
FSC® C018179

Set in 15/17 Garamond MT

Red Fox Books are published by Random House Children's Publishers UK
61–63 Uxbridge Road, London W5 5SA

www.randomhousechildrensbooks.co.uk
www.totallyrandombooks.co.uk
www.randomhouse.co.uk

Addresses for companies within The Random House Group Limited can be found at:
www.randomhouse.co.uk/offices.htm

THE RANDOM HOUSE GROUP Limited Reg. No. 954009

A CIP catalogue record for this book is available from the British Library.

Printed and bound in Great Britain by Clays Ltd, St Ives plc

NAME: Charlie Small

ADDRESS: Planet of the Gerks

AGE: 400 years, and counting!

MOBILE: 07713

SCHOOL: What's school?

THINGS I LIKE: Philly and her mum and dad; Mad Dog and Pod!

THINGS I HATE: Gerks — every single one of 'em; Gravitator (it landed me in so much trouble!); Joseph Craik (the meanest man in the whole wide world)

NAME
ADDRESS
AGE

If you find this book, - PLEASE - look after it. This is the ONLY true account of my remarkable adventures.

My name is Charlie Small and I am four hundred years old. But in all those long years I have never grown up. Something happened when I was eight years old, something I can't begin to understand. I went on a journey . . . and I'm still trying to find my way home. Now, although I've travelled across space to unknown planets, been hunted by revolting, reptilian Gerks and narrowly avoided having my brain hoovered, I still look like any eight-year-old boy you might pass in the street.

I've escaped certain hanging and defeated a whole city of aliens! You may think this sounds fantastic; you could think it's a lie. But you would be wrong, because EVERYTHING IN THIS BOOK IS TRUE. Believe this single fact and you can share the most incredible journey ever experienced.

Charlie Small

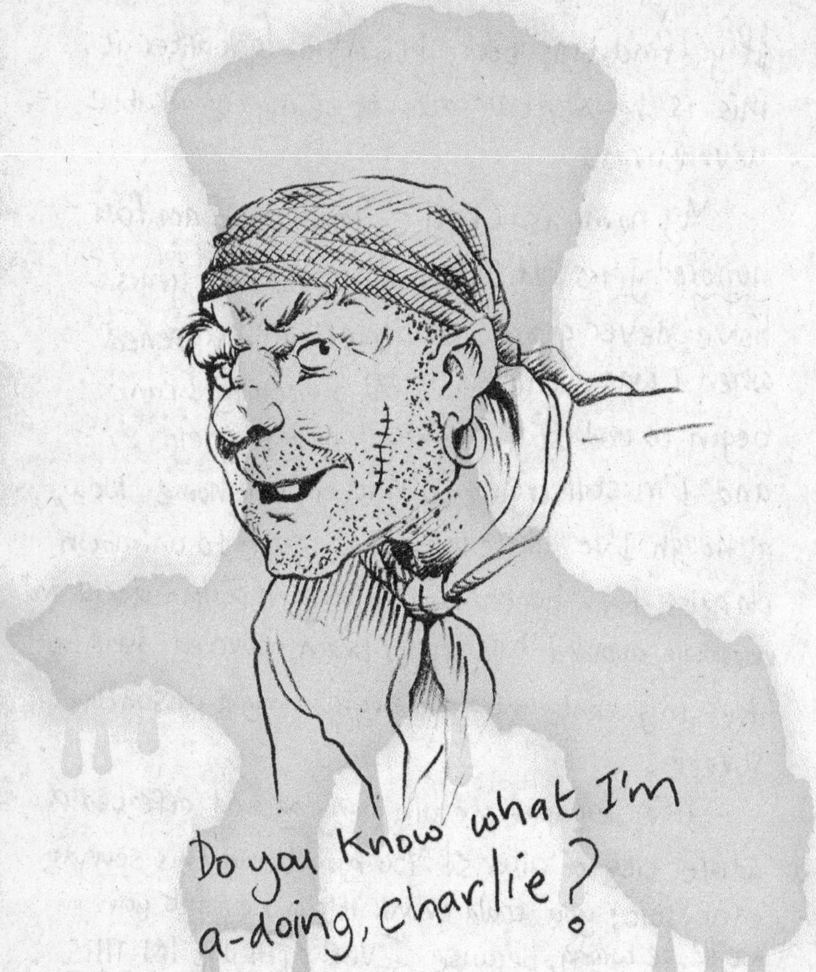
Do you know what I'm a-doing, Charlie?

Hanging Around!

BANG! CRASH! THUMP!

'Do you know what I'm a-doing, Charlie Small?' came Joseph Craik's voice from outside.

I could hear him, but the barred window in my cell was too high for me to see. Even so, I knew exactly what the old reprobate was up to. I didn't answer, though. It would only make him gloat even more.

'I'm makin' some gallows, Charlie, just for you,' came his sneering voice. 'I could use my mobile noose, but now I've managed to capture you I've decided to do the job properly and build a really solid gibbet. I think you'll like it, Charlie. Hee, hee!'

Then the despicable thief-taker broke into a sinister gallows song:

'You should see them a-wriggling on the rope,
They wriggle even when there is no hope,
Yes, you should see them wriggle
It would really make you giggle,
To see them a-croaking on the rope.'

I looked around my cell for the hundredth time but I still couldn't see a way out. It looked as though Craik had finally defeated me. To think that this time two days ago, I had finally managed to get back home after being away for four hundred years!

Return To The Land Of Adventure

(see my Journal Forest Of Skulls)

My dad and I had escaped from the Forest of Skulls by squeezing into a hollow tree and following a tunnel that led all the way to my back garden. It felt great to be home after such a long time and I was really looking forward to some of Mum's cooking – I'd been living on worms and gristly grubs for far too long! But I didn't get to taste anything, and I didn't even get to sleep in my own bed!

Mum asked me to get some milk from the corner shop, and on the way home I bumped headlong into Craik, my very worst enemy. I've no idea how he managed to find his way into my world, but he'd promised to track me to the ends of the earth and he was keeping his word! The bullying bandit manhandled me through town. I struggled and yelled but it was like walking through a DVD on pause – every person in the street had frozen as though time had stopped still.

Craik took me to the canal, shoved me aboard a decaying narrowboat and chained me to the tiller. The bully then steered the boat into a disused arm of the waterway. The banks were overgrown with brambles and weeds and eventually we came to a narrow tunnel that took the canal through a dome-shaped hill. The entrance was boarded up but Craik yanked the planks apart and steered the boat inside.

The canal went into a tunnel in a dome-shaped hill

Almost instantly we were whisked along on a really fast current. The sides of the narrowboat banged and scraped along the tunnel walls sending sparks arcing into the air. The waters roared; metal screamed against brick, filling the air with a deafening noise that jarred in my ears. Just as I thought I could stand it no longer, our boat crashed through another set of boards and we burst out into bright sunlight.

I shielded my eyes; then, as the coloured lights that swam across them subsided, I glanced around me. Everything seemed somehow brighter and sharper; almost dream-like, and I instinctively knew I'd been taken back to the strange and dangerous world of my adventures!

A few miles down river, Craik moored the boat to a wooden jetty at the bottom of a sloping, overgrown garden. A path led up to a large, dark, turretted mansion.

'Welcome to my humble abode,' sneered Craik, and undoing the chains he grabbed me by my collar and dragged me up the garden path. I was shoved inside a small, dusty room built onto the back of the main house, and the heavy oak door was slammed and locked behind me.

My Very Last Entry — Ever!

That was two days ago. Since then I've been trapped in this stinking hole with just a few mice for company, and had to sleep on a pile of smelly straw. Craik has only given me a mug of rancid water and some bread and dripping to eat.

Hey, mice are good company!

I've searched high and low for a way out, but Craik is a professional thief-taker and the stronghold seems escape-proof. I tested the floor to see if I could dig a tunnel, but it's made of solid concrete and my penknife blade doesn't even scratch the surface. The one window is high up in the brick wall and has a row of heavy iron bars right the way across. *Darn it!* I thought. *Surely there's got to be a way out somewhere.*

I shall check in my rucksack to see if it will spark any ideas. I never go anywhere without my precious explorer's kit (not even to the corner shop, thank goodness!) — it has helped me loads of times on my adventures, and if anyone who reads this ever wants to do some exploring, remember to make sure you take a bag full of useful things!

My rucksack now contains:

1) My multi-tooled penknife
2) A ball of string
3) A water bottle
4) A telescope
5) A scarf (complete with bullet holes!)
6) An old railway ticket
7) This journal

My rucksack

If you find this boy
somewhere it is a mystery
Charlie
Small
boy adventures

Thrak is a
great hairy
twit!

The Charlie Sm

PLANET

Joseph
Craik is
a wimp!

Captain
Cut-throat
is a no-good
low-down thief!

Down
with Baby

8) A pack of wild animal collectors cards (full of amazing animal facts)

9) A glue pen to stick things in my notebook

10) A glass eye from my brave steam-powered rhinoceros friend

11) The compass and torch I found on the sun-bleached skeleton of a lost explorer (I managed to mend the torch's winder which broke in the Underworld)

12) The tooth of a monstrous megashark (makes a handy saw)

13) A magnifying glass (for starting fires etc)

14) A radio

15) My mobile phone with wind-up charger

16) The skull of a Barbarous Bat (broken by Barcus the badger's big flat feet!)

17) A bundle of maps and diagrams (showing many of the places I have travelled)

18) A bag of marbles

19) A plastic lemon full of lemon juice

20) A lasso

21) The bony finger of an animated skeleton

22) The little box that Philly gave me (see my journal *The Forest of Skulls*)

All of these things have been useful to me,

but for the first time ever on my adventures I can't come up with a single plan. I am well and truly stuck in Craik's grisly den, waiting for him to finish his deadly DIY project.

Hours And Hours Later

My time is up! I can hear Craik fumbling with his keys outside my prison door and I'm about to be taken to the gallows to hang. Oh yikes! After all this time and all my adventures, I never thought it would end like this. Being skewered on the end of Captain Cut-throat's cutlass maybe, but to be nabbed by the snivelling sneak Craik is almost too much to bear. I'll finish my journal here. Goodbye, cruel world!

Escape — Yahoo!

You won't believe it! I didn't hang! And now I'm miles beyond Craik's reach. Let me explain how I got away.

As Craik opened the cell door, I refilled my rucksack and lifted it onto my back.

'That won't be much good to you where you're goin',' sneered Craik as he led me around the corner of the dark mansion to where a large gallows stood in the middle of a cobbled yard.

It was miserable weather. A strong breeze whipped across the courtyard and a layer of soggy, grey clouds sat so low in the sky they almost touched the tops of the skeletal trees in Craik's garden. A few cold raindrops splashed against my face.

'OK, up you go,' said Craik, pushing me towards the steps that led to a high platform.

'Make sure you don't trip – I wouldn't want you to hurt yourself. Hee, hee, hee!'

'Very funny,' I croaked. My mouth had gone dry and my heart banged like a kettledrum as I stepped onto the platform, but I wasn't going to let Craik see I was scared. He followed behind me, rubbing his rough, stubby-fingered hands in delight.

'Stand there, please,' he said, pointing to a spot where I could see the faint outline of a trapdoor. He had become very polite in his excitement at finally seeing me off! 'That's right, well done. Now, if you wouldn't mind just slipping this around your neck.' He lifted the heavy noose that dangled from the crossbar above my head, presenting it to me as if it were a valuable gift. 'Don't be shy, just duck your head a bit, that's it . . . 'Ello, what's that noise?'

There was a loud pinging sound coming from somewhere.

'It's something in your rucksack,' cried Craik. 'What is it?'

'I've no idea!' I said. There was nothing in my bag that made a noise like that. It certainly wasn't the ring-tone on my mobile.

'Turn it off, you blighter,' demanded Craik,

dropping the noose. 'What tricks are you up to now?'

'I'm not up to any tricks, honest,' I said, letting my rucksack slip to the floor.

Craik tore open the bag, rummaging around inside. 'What's this?' he demanded, holding up a small wooden box that was pinging like a microwave.

'It's just an empty box,' I said, staring at the little gift Philly had given me when Captain Cut-throat had carted me away from Jakeman's factory. I was amazed – the box had never made a noise before.

'I don't believe you,' said Craik suspiciously. Then the pinging got louder and the box began to rattle and vibrate in his hand. 'It's a bomb!' he screamed, and threw it across the yard into a muddy puddle as he dived flat onto the platform, covering his stubbly head with his arms.

At that very moment, something whacked me in the back and I span round. Imagine my shock, surprise and delight when I saw a long

A rope ladder whacked me on the back

rope ladder dangling from the low, grey clouds above, jiggling and swaying in the wind!

'Yahoo!' I yelled, and I scooped up my rucksack, grabbed the bottom rung and started to climb.

'No! Come back here,' bellowed Craik scrabbling to his feet and lunging at me.

'Not on your nelly!' I cried.

I kicked out, catching him a blow on the shoulder and, like the trained monkey I was, scrambled up the swinging ladder. The moment I started to climb, the rope ladder was hoisted into the air and I was lost amongst the sodden clouds. It was only then that I began to wonder where it might have come from – had I jumped out of a frying pan and into a fire? I might be lifted straight into the jaws of a hungry monster!

I could still hear Craik bellowing as I emerged through the top of the cloud into bright sunlight. I glanced up, just in time to see that I was being lifted through a dark hatchway – a hatchway that appeared to be let into the sky itself. The hatch closed silently below me and I found myself in complete darkness.

Guess Who!

I held my breath and listened. It was deathly quiet. I could no longer make out Craik's yelling from below; there was no sound of the whistling wind. All I could hear was my own blood pumping through my body.

I began to get nervous. Where had I ended up? Perhaps I was inside some sort of monster? Then there was a clatter that nearly gave me a heart attack, and a square of light opened just above my head. A freckly, smiling face peered down at me.

'Philly!' I cried. It was Jakeman's granddaughter who had become one of my very best friends on our adventures beyond the Great Divide.

'Are you going to stay down there all day?' she grinned and held a hand down to me. I grabbed hold of it and Philly pulled me out of the black hole and into a shining, pale blue cabin.

'Philly, what are you doing here?' I cried as we gave each other a huge hug.

'I came to rescue you,' she said, smiling.

'But, how did you find me?' I asked.

'By the box, silly,' said Philly.

'The box?' I said, starting to feel confused.

'The little forget-me-not box I gave you at Grandpa's factory. Surely you realized it was a homing device?' Philly said, crossing her arms and raising her eyebrows. 'We've tracked you ever since, but it's only now that we've been able to get an invention ready to come and rescue you.'

It was Philly!

'Oh, it was a *homing* device,' I said, understanding at last.

'Why else would I give you a present?' said Philly, laughing.

Just then there was a loud scrabbling noise from behind one of the steel walls; an automatic door swished silently open and Mad Dog,

(See my journal The Mummy's Tomb)

It was Mad Dog!

the crazy mechanical canine we found at the Mummy's Tomb, came clattering into the room. When he saw me, he started barking metallically and wagging his tungsten tail.

'Mad Dog!' I cried delightedly, bending down to pat his leathery back. 'You're here as well! Where's Jakeman?'

'Oh, he's back at the factory,' explained Philly. 'Someone had to stay behind and look after things. He said I was more than capable of handling this mission myself, and I'm so much better at piloting the Gravitator than him. Talk about a careful driver – Gramps would never have caught up with you!'

'So you're completely on your own?' I asked.

'Yeah, apart from Mad Dog – but I keep in touch with Gramps on my mobile,' said Philly.

'So, is this the Gravitator we're in now?' I asked, looking around the cabin. The walls curved around us – it was like being inside a huge blue egg.

'Sure is,' said Philly. 'Come on, I'll show you where everything is.'

The Gravitator

The room we were in was quite large and
the shiny, pale blue walls were smooth and
featureless. Apart from a flat, oval TV monitor

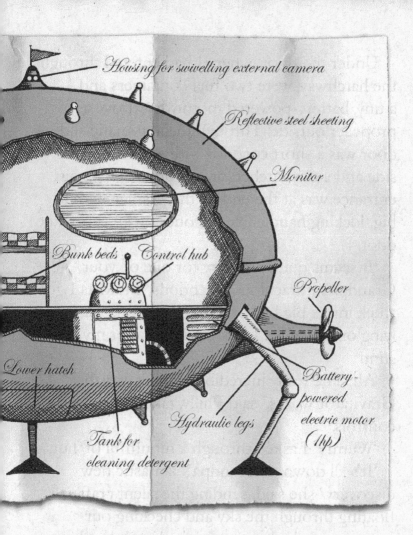

Housing for swivelling external camera

Reflective steel sheeting

Monitor

Bunk beds

Control hub

Propeller

Lower hatch

Battery-powered electric motor (1hp)

Hydraulic legs

Tank for cleaning detergent

on one wall and a simple control hub below it, there were two chairs, two bunkbeds and a small fold-down table, all made from the same gleaming, bluish metal. Tiny pinpricks of light flashed across the ceiling in sequence.

Under the floor, where I had entered through the hatchway, were two fuel containers and a tiny, battery-powered motor that drove a propeller outside. Through the automatic sliding door was a short corridor with a toilet on one side and a tiny kitchen on the other. The main entrance was at the end of the passage with a big, locking handle like the ones on an aeroplane door.

'It seems quite ordinary for one of your Grandpa's miraculous inventions,' I said as I got stuck into a big bag of roasted peanuts that was lying on the table. I was famished after my jail stint!

'Ah! The really incredible thing is *how* the Gravitator works,' said Philly, taking the controls.

'Wumf?' I asked through a mouthful of nuts.

'It's all down to Grandpa's fantastic new discovery,' she said, sending the silent craft floating through the sky and checking our progress on the large monitor that showed a moving image of the world outside. 'A little while ago, when he was mixing liquids in the lab and heating them over a Bunsen burner, a quite remarkable chemical reaction took place.

He added some crystallized cuckoo spit to a
concoction he had on the boil, and the liquid
foamed up like bubble bath. Then the foaming
liquid floated out of the jar and across the
room! Gramps pretended he knew it was going
to happen all along, but, as he chased the liquid
blob around the room, a bit splashed against
his old cap, which lifted off his
head and floated away. This
time Grandpa couldn't hide
his amazement, because he
realized he'd just invented an
anti-gravity liquid! Well, to cut
a long story short, Grandpa
added the stuff to a special, non-
drying paint. By spraying the outside of the craft
with it, we can float high in the sky.'

Grandpa's cap floated across the room!

'So, we're flying by the power of anti-gravity
paint?' I exclaimed, nearly choking on the
peanuts.

'That's right, and I can control our height
with this lever,' said Philly. 'If I push it forward,
a network of small nozzles sprays the outside of
the craft with a fine mist of extra liquid, and . . .
up we go!' Philly thrust the lever forward and we
shot straight up into the sky.

'GOING UP,' crackled a tinny voice from the onboard computer. 'ONE THOUSAND FEET, TWO THOUSAND FEET . . .'

Whoa! It was like being in a super-fast lift, and I stumbled, spilling the bag of peanuts all over the floor.

'Oh Charlie,' cried Philly. 'They'll take ages to clear up!' She pulled the lever and we floated back down to our original cruising height.

'GOING DOWN,' said the voice.

'Pulling the lever this way sprays the outside with hot, soapy water which washes off some of the anti-gravity liquid, so we drop down,' explained Philly. 'Come on, I'll help you clear up this mess.'

Breakdown

'So how come I didn't see the Gravitator when you first rescued me?' I asked as we scrabbled around picking up peanuts from the cabin floor. 'All I saw was the dark open hatchway. It looked like a door into the sky!'

'That's because Grandpa's paint has millions of highly reflective crystals in it that reflect the colour of the sky, making the Gravitator virtually invisible,' explained Philly. 'It's great, although it does mean it can be a bit tricky to find sometimes. I've fitted a little flag on the roof to make it easier to see when it's parked on the ground.'

'It's incredible,' I said, watching the landscape whip along below us on the monitor. 'And that little engine in the hold is powerful enough to drive us along at this speed?'

'Oh, easily,' said Philly. 'Because we weigh virtually nothing. It's a very eco-friendly form of transport.'

The layer of grey clouds had dispersed now and I could see we were flying above a region of flat, rocky plateaus.

'How far is it to the factory?' I asked.

'Not too far. You'll just have time to tell me what you've been up to since Cut-throat kidnapped you,' said Philly, steering the Gravitator with a small wheel on top of the control hub. 'Go and put the kettle on and you can tell me all about it over a cup of tea.'

The little steering wheel

I made a pot of tea in the little kitchen, grabbed a packet of squashed fly biscuits, and rushed back to the cabin.

'You won't *believe* the adventure I've had,' I began, sitting down at the fold-up table as Philly drank her tea at the controls. I started to tell her all about the whale, the Forest of Skulls, the badger and rat war, and meeting up with my dad – but I had only got halfway through my tale when, *Grrnnzz!* the control hub gave a horrible grinding noise, and we started drifting towards the ground.

'I don't like the sound of that!' exclaimed Philly. She pushed and pulled at the altitude lever, but apart from giving another ear-piercing screech, it didn't do anything. We continued to descend.

'Something's jammed the lever,' she said. 'I can't make us climb again. We'd better land and have a look.'

Take Off!

We waited until the Gravitator gently floated from the sky and landed on a plateau. Philly got her toolkit and unscrewed the side of the control hub. Peering at the wires and workings inside she tutted and poked about with the end of her screwdriver.

'Well, something's jamming it, but I'll be blowed if I can see what!' she said. 'I'd better have a look in the access panel outside. Maybe a bit of grit has got caught up in the linkage chain.' Taking her screwdriver, she opened the main door, tipped out a folding flight of steps and climbed down. Mad Dog remained inside, looking quizzically up at me.

'Nothing to worry about, old chap,' I said, giving the mechanical dog a pat.

I could hear Philly clattering about outside and I wandered back into the cabin.

Typical, I thought. Only a few miles from Jakeman's and this has to happen. Still, we should be on our way soon. I gave the lever a rattle, then crouched down and had a look inside.

Hello, I thought. *What's that?* I got the torch from my explorer's kit and shone it inside. There was something stuck right in the elbow of a joint in the lever. I gave the side of the control box a whack. Nothing happened. I gave it a harder smack, and a lone peanut rolled out across the floor!

This is the guilty peanut ↓

Whoops! Looks like it might have been my fault all along. Best not let Philly know… I ate the evidence and grabbed hold of the lever. *I'll check it has freed up*, I thought to myself and pushed at the handle. It was still very stiff. *Must be a bit of peanut still caught*, I thought and gave the lever a harder shove. *CLANG!* The handle jolted forward and the Gravitator rocketed up in the air!

Whoosh! I was knocked to the floor as we climbed at the speed of a jet fighter.

'GOING UP,' said the computer. 'ONE THOUSAND FEET . . .'

'Oh yikes!' I cried. 'Philly, help!' But Philly had been left on the ground!

'Waoow!' whined Mad Dog, running around in panic.

I got to my feet and grabbed the lever. Now it had become loose, flopping about uselessly, and I couldn't put the Gravitator into descend mode!

'TWO THOUSAND FEET AND STILL CLIMBING,' the voice calmly informed me.

Oh, brilliant, what now? I wondered.

Whoosh!

To The Edge Of Space And Beyond! ✦

The sliding door was opening and closing, over and over, *sweesh, sweesh*. Wind whipped down the corridor, and papers, cups, sheets and pillows – anything that wasn't bolted down – went flying from the cabin and were sucked along the passage and out of the main door.

'WARNING, DOOR NOT SECURED! WARNING, DOOR NOT SECURED!'

The Gravitator rocked and juddered in an alarming fashion. I had to get the main door closed before all the rivets rattled loose and we fell to bits in mid air!

I struggled along the passage, fighting the buffeting wind, and managed to grab the door handle. Whoa! My legs were whipped from under me and I was sucked out of the door. Still holding the handle with one hand, I flapped around in the slipstream like a flag.

'Help!' I yelled, wind whistling round my ears. I knew I couldn't hold on for long.

'FIVE THOUSAND FEET AND CLIMBING,' the tinny speaker announced.

'Give us a hand,' I bellowed above the

screaming gale and Mad Dog crawled to the very edge of the doorway and wedged his paws behind the doorjamb.

You'll never reach me, I thought. Then, to my amazement, the metal mutt's neck started to extend like a telescope! Inch by inch it got longer and longer until his broad head was level with mine. Then, striking like some sort of weird snake, he grabbed the collar of my top with his strong, steel teeth.

He was just in time. My grip gave way and I would have hurtled to the ground below, but my canine friend held fast, slowly retracting his neck and dragging me back on to the floor of the flying machine. I pushed against the door with my feet; Mad Dog used his powerful head – we struggled and fought until, eventually, the lock clicked into place, the noise of the wind was shut out and the Gravitator stopped rocking.

I slipped to the floor. 'Thanks, Mad Dog,' I said, wiping a sheen of sweat from my brow. But we were still in big trouble. We continued to zoom up through the air like a runaway rocket! I staggered back into the cabin, just in time to hear a low hissing noise coming from the cabin walls.

'EMERGENCY AIR SUPPLY ON,' said the Gravitator.

Wow, we must be getting really high, I thought and stared up at the monitor. All of a sudden it filled with snowy interference and a few minutes later our craft started to shake like a boiling kettle. I struggled over to one of the chairs and sat down, holding onto the seat with both hands. The rattling grew and grew and my chair started to judder across the floor.

'DANGER, REDUCE CRUISING-HEIGHT IMMEDIATELY!'

'Help!' I yelled.

'Owww!' howled Mad Dog.

It felt like we were being shaken to pieces! Then, all of a sudden the juddering stopped and there was complete silence. The snowy monitor cleared and went black. I was just beginning to think it had completely broken, when a streak of fire arced across the screen.

What the heck was that? I wondered. Then I noticed that the black screen was dotted with tiny spots of light, and I realized where I was. The streak of fire was an asteroid; the hard dots of light were stars.

'POSITION DOES NOT COMPUTE,' announced the speaker.

I must be in SPACE! Yikes!

Stuck In Space!

I jiggled the lever on the control box again. It was completely useless. Anyway, even if it did work it wouldn't be any good now. There is no gravity in space, so an anti-gravity craft would be pointless. I couldn't even turn the Gravitator around and head back to earth, as the little steering wheel span uselessly round and round.

Jeepers creepers! The craft's initial thrust had sent us rocketing across space at incredible speed; there were no brakes and it wouldn't stop until it reached the edge of space. Forget being four hundred years old – unless I can repair the Gravitator myself, I could be stuck out here for four *thousand* years!

Suddenly I had a worrying thought. Philly and Jakeman would have only loaded the Gravitator with enough supplies for their rescue mission, not for a journey into space! I ran into the kitchen and opened the cupboard doors. Oh, great! This is what I had to sustain me in space:

One bottle of pop (flat)
One can of sardines (out of date)
One curry-flavoured pot of dried noodles (excellent)
One bar of chocolate
(three-quarters eaten – thanks, Philly!)

'It's a good job you don't need feeding,' I said to my mechanical pooch. 'Otherwise we'd be in real trouble.'

I stared up at the big monitor. The black sky was strewn with tiny silver stars and, right in the middle of the screen, was planet earth. It shone like a beautiful blue marble in the vastness of space and was getting smaller and smaller by the minute. *Jeepers*, I thought, *maybe I'll be the thirteenth person to ever land on the moon.* Talk about the ultimate adventure! But then I saw the moon appear on the screen, and soon that too had been left far behind and I realized I was going much further than any of the Apollo astronauts ever had. Yikes!

I have to do something. I don't want to travel to the end of infinity in this glorified tin can. The only thing I can think of is to take the control box to bits and try to fix the steering mechanism so I can at least turn the craft around.

Now I've been racing through space for six hours. I've laid out the control-box workings on the floor – it looks like a bolt has sheared and a connecting belt around some wheels has snapped. I might just be able to mend it, but not tonight. All of a sudden I've come over really tired and dizzy. Maybe it's the effect of being in space, but I can hardly keep my eyes open.

I'll just finish these notes, and then get some shut-eye. I wonder where Philly is now? I hope she made it back to Jakeman's factory all right. Huh! She's probably tucked up in a warm, squashy bed with a mug of hot cocoa, while I'm trying to get comfy on this hard bunkbed with no covers or pillow, and sipping on flat, tepid cola! Added to that my mechanical mutt is curled up at my feet wheezing and whirring like an old boiler. Goodnight!

Attack Of The Starfish

I always thought space was called space because there's nothing in it – well it can't be, because there are *loads* of things floating around up here, and I had my first, deadly close encounter this morning!

I finished the noodle pot for breakfast and was about to start putting the control box back together. I had found a replacement for the broken bolt in Philly's toolbox and cut a length of string from the ball in my rucksack. If I tied it in a loop it could act as a substitute for the drive belt. Mad Dog was sitting next to me, staring at my attempts at being a mechanic with his head tilted to one side, when all of a sudden there was a strange noise, *splat*, which shook the metal cabin.

I stared at the monitor, but apart from a cluster of stars up ahead I couldn't see anything. Then I noticed the stars were getting bigger; they looked as though they were coming straight towards us! They glowed green and purple and as they got closer I saw the things had horrible round mouths, right in the middle. A set of saw-like gnashers protruded from between big, sucker-like lips. These were no stars – they were some type of alien intergalactic starfish, the size of bicycle wheels!

Kersplat! We were hit again. *Splat, splot, flump!* The Gravitator rocked like a cradle, and the workings of the control box, all the screws, washers, pins and pinions that I'd carefully lined up on the floor, went rolling over the deck. I could hear the clinking sound as some of them dropped down a grill that ran round the edge of the cabin. *Oh brilliant,* I thought, *now I'm really up the creek without a paddle!*

Using a remote control that sat in a holster on the side of the monitor, I turned the external camera, and the lens swept around to point down at the Gravitator's hull. The starfish were stuck to it like great blobs of jelly.

Then I heard a horrible grating noise and realized they were starting to eat into the metal with their saw-like teeth. Oh, jeepers, if they pierced the craft, all the air would escape and I'd be done for! I ran into the kitchen and rifled through the cupboards, throwing useless knives and forks, bits of fuse wire and pencil stubs on the floor. At last I found something that might help: Jakeman's instruction booklet for the Gravitator.

Frying Tonight!

As the grinding noise
from outside got
louder, and more
starfish landed on the hull,
I hurriedly flicked through the
pages and scanned the headings:

Splat!

Starting the Motor – no good
Using the Anti-gravity Lever – I haven't got
one any more!
Cooking Facilities – oh, come on, there must
be *something* useful in here
**Why You Should Never Take the Gravitator
Higher than Twenty Thousand Feet** –
Oh, now I find out this thing wasn't even
designed to go into space!
Heating System – what good is that? Hold on,
though . . . I sat down and rapidly read through
the chapter on the Gravitator's central heating.
It worked by heating up the fuselage, and there
was a warning highlighted in a separate panel:
Outside surfaces may get very hot to the touch. Yes, that
might do it!

I located the thermostat inside a kitchen cupboard and flicked it up to FULL. Then I sat back and waited, praying that the starfish's teeth were blunter than they looked. It didn't take long, and within a couple of minutes the cabin started to heat up. Within five minutes it was getting positively tropical, and I had to take off my top. A few minutes later and I was sitting in just my underpants, sweat running down my back, and Mad Dog looking at me as if I'd gone completely bonkers!

I was sitting in just my underpants!

On the monitor I could see the space starfish start to squirm as the fuselage got hotter and hotter. They lifted their arms, one by one, in an attempt to cool themselves down. The chewing noise stopped and as the heat became too much, some of the starfish dropped away with little bird-like squeals. The stubborn ones remained until, in a sudden plume of smoke, they were griddled like steaks on a barbie!

With a sigh of relief I turned the thermostat down, and a few minutes later got dressed as the temperature started to drop. It was a pity I'd had no way of catching the burrowing blighters

– barbecued starfish might be quite tasty!

If I thought my immediate problems were over, though, I was wrong.

All of a sudden there was another almighty crash. The cabin vibrated like an alarm clock going off and a big dent appeared in the ceiling. *BOOM!* I quickly scanned the void outside. Oh yikes! Rocketing, red-hot rocks zipped all around us. We had flown directly into a deadly meteorite storm.

Mad Dog whined as the Gravitator was hit from all sides, knocking it this way and that. The walls became pitted with dents – and there was nothing I could do about it. I couldn't steer us away from the storm. We were at the mercy of the elements. Now I know what it would be like to be shaken about inside one of those plastic snowstorm ornaments.

We hunkered down on the floor; I held on to the leg of one of the bunks to stop myself being thrown around the cabin and Mad Dog buried his head in my lap, shivering in fear. I prayed the Gravitator would hold as we were swatted across space like an annoying fly.

Then, as quickly as it had started, everything went quiet. Remarkably, since the Gravitator was never designed for space travel, we had weathered the storm.

'We made it, Mad Dog,' I cried, giving him a hug. 'Now let's try and retrieve all the bits of the control box and get it fixed.' Just then, though, I felt the Gravitator change direction. 'Hello, what the heck's happening now?' I said. There was no doubt about it; I could feel the Gravitator being pulled away to the left as if we had strayed too close to a giant magnet.

I moved the remote camera again, until it was peering across space in the direction we were being pulled, and gasped in horror. There, looming like a great, swirling, gaseous orange, was a massive planet – and we were obviously in the grip of its gravitational field.

'Oh, yikes!' I cried. 'Now we're for it, Mad Dog.' For, like it or not, we were going to make an unscheduled stop!

A swirling, gaseous planet

Crash Landing

We raced towards the enormous globe in a huge sweeping arc. Again the monitor snowed up, crackling and popping as we bumpily entered the planet's atmosphere – and then we were through. The screen slowly cleared, and displayed a panorama of folding hills and yellow mountains. I could make out blue forests and huge sheets of ice-white water.

'GOING DOWN. TWENTY THOUSAND FEET; FIFTEEN THOUSAND FEET...' said the onboard computer.

Why aren't we floating? I wondered. Perhaps the starfish had rubbed off all our anti-gravitation paint. We continued to drop until we were amongst the rounded peaks of a range of hills, shooting along like a guided missile.

'WARNING! WARNING! WATCH OUT, WE'RE GOING TO CRASH!' yelled the computer, getting quite agitated.

'Brace yourself, Mad Dog,' I yelled.

BOOM! We hit the ground and I was thrown straight up, cracking my head on the ceiling. We rebounded from the ground and then, *BOOM!* we hit it again. We bounced and span for miles, like a cricket ball hit for six. Then, rolling over and over, we finally came to a stop. The Gravitator rocked slightly, and then was still.

'OH, MARVELLOUS! YOU'VE ONLY GONE AND CRASHED,' said the computer accusingly.

'Aaoow!' howled Mad Dog, crouching on the floor in fear.

'Don't worry, boy,' I said, giving him a reassuring pat. 'It's all over. Now, though, I've got to find out if I can breathe in the atmosphere outside. If I can't, it's curtains for me. You should be all right being a robot. Thing is, how do I find out if I can breathe out there, without going outside? The air might be pure poison!'

Crash! With a shudder and a clatter of falling

steel, the whole Gravitator collapsed about me, and I found myself standing in the open air amongst a pile of shattered metal.

'That's one way of finding out, I suppose,' I said, breathing in a huge lungful of air.

I'm glad to report that I didn't keel over gripping my throat and gurgling in agony! The air was very damp and warm, and smelled rather like a stagnant pond, but it wasn't too bad.

'Well, at least I can breathe,' I said to Mad Dog, picking up my explorer's kit from under the remains of the bunkbeds. I gave a long, slow sigh as I looked at the wreckage. There was nothing left of the Gravitator's motor, or the propeller. The fuel tanks had split open and the anti-gravity mixture was floating off into the sky.

'What now?' I murmured, knowing I was well and truly stuck. 'I suppose we'd better find some sort of shelter in case there are any alien marauders around.' Then, as my tummy gave a loud rumbling gurgle, I added, 'And let's see if there's anything edible on this planet.'

My First Night On The Orange Planet

I'm holed up in a cave in the side of a small hill and night is approaching. There doesn't seem to be a setting sun, but the clear, bright sky has dimmed to a dull glow, as if a celestial lamp has been turned down low. The planet is completely silent; I haven't seen sight nor sound of any monsters or aliens. There are no flying creatures in the sky, nothing perched in the strange, blue trees which have curly and twisty branches like tangled string.

I found a cave in the rolling hills

I haven't found anything to eat either, and had to go back to the wreck of the Gravitator to salvage the tin of sardines. I also brought away the dregs of the pop bottle and some of Philly's tools in case they should come in handy.

Walking is the weirdest experience on this

planet. It's not the same as the moon, where there is less gravity and you can leap twenty feet without even trying. The gravity seems the same as it is on earth – but when I stepped away from the rubble of my craft, my foot sank halfway up to my knees! The ground is soft and springy; it's like walking on a trampoline or a giant marshmallow, and is very tiring. It took me ages to cover the half mile to this line of low hills, which I thought might offer me some cover from prying eyes. Luckily, as I neared the hills the ground firmed up into a hard, dusty rock and I began to walk normally.

The planet has a distinct orange tinge that seems to colour the air, and when the light in the sky is bright, it's like looking through a sheet of orange perspex. Everything is covered with a slimy film of moisture from the clammy air and my clothes have become horribly damp and clingy.

I have spent a number of hours checking out my surroundings, but there isn't much to see. The silent hills fold away into the distance and on the horizon I can see the blur of a blue forest.

Have I ever been in a worse situation? I don't

think so: I'm trapped on an unknown planet, light-years away from home, with no company apart from one rather daft robotic dog. My tummy is growling with hunger and I reckon I'm going to be lucky to survive! I've asked the faithful Mad Dog to stand guard whilst I get some sleep. I hope things look better in the morning.

Eggy-Bread Fruit

I awoke to a bright, brand new day. Checking the clock on my mobile I saw I'd been asleep for nearly ten hours! Gone was the orangey glow of yesterday, instead the early morning light gave everything a pale, lemony yellow luminescence. The air was still heavy with moisture, but much fresher, and I felt positive and ready for action.

The first thing I did was to try to contact Mum on my mobile. I wanted to check she was OK after my surprise trip home. I've often phoned her on my adventures but when I've managed to get through, the conversation has always been the same. She always expects me back in time for tea, even though I've been gone for four hundred years! Would it be the same now? I punched in the numbers, pressed call and waited – nothing. Darn it, I wasn't going to find out how she was – there was no blooming signal!

Oh well, I thought, *I'll try another time.* Gulping down the last of the cold, slippery sardines, I put on my rucksack and went out to explore.

As soon as I left the hills the ground became springy and soft again, so I climbed back and followed a hard, raised ridge of rock that took me on a sweeping curve. I knew I could easily find my way home to the cave by following the ridge back again, so I stepped out confidently. Mad Dog ran at my side, his steel tail whirring like an electric whisk.

It wasn't long before the damp air had soaked into my clothes and my hair was plastered down on my forehead. It was horrible, and I began to wonder if I would eventually start to develop gills!

Then, at the bottom of one of the hills I saw a group of purple bushes and, hanging from the branches was a cluster of large, shiny teardrop shapes. *Fruit!* I thought, *or maybe giant nuts!* I scrambled down and, with my penknife, cut one

of the crimson globes from a branch. I sliced
into the juicy flesh. It was bright red inside and
looked a bit like a melon. It smelled delicious
and I tentatively took a bite . . . Yum, yum!

I saw some teardrop-shaped
fruit, yum yum!

I know I should have waited to see if I
developed a tummy ache or threw up, or started
to see weird shapes in the sky, but I was so
hungry I couldn't help myself, and I greedily
carried on until I'd scoffed the whole thing
down.

'It's delicious,' I said to Mad Dog with a satisfying burp. 'It tastes just like eggy bread!' I was very relieved; one of my immediate problems had been solved – I wasn't going to starve!

I cut another fruit open and ate that. This was greener inside and had a cheesy flavour, but was still really tasty, so I picked some more and jammed them into my rucksack. 'Come on, Mad Dog,' I called to the metal mutt who was sniffing at the discarded fruit skin. 'Let's find out if this planet is inhabited. If so, maybe they will help me build a new spacecraft and get home!'

One Week Later

We've found nothing so far and I'm beginning to get a bit concerned. Is this it? Maybe I'm really going to stay on this deserted damp dump, with no one to talk to but a mechanical pet until I become an old, bearded loon. It's great to have Mad Dog with me; I reckon I'd already be a gibbering wreck if it wasn't for his company, but he's not the greatest conversationalist ever!

He doesn't come up with any plans – though to be fair he did sniff out a new batch of fruit for me today.

A gibbering wreck!

Two Weeks Later

Still no sightings of any living creature, and I'm starting to go a bit doolally. I have discovered one of the white lakes I spotted from the sky, and filled up the bottle in my explorer's kit. It tastes delicious – icy, clear, sweet-tasting water just like a slushy.

I started trying to rebuild the Gravitator, but I've given it up as a lost cause – what was a perfect egg shape now looks more like half a gnarled old potato, and without a motor or the anti-gravity device, it's nothing more than an empty shell.

I have begun to make my cave more cosy, though. With the Megashark's tooth from my explorer's kit, I sawed out a large rectangle of the squashy ground and dragged it up here for a mattress. It's very comfy! On one of my walks, I found a strange, bright yellow flower that turns its face towards me at the sound of my voice, and I've put it in the empty coke bottle on a rocky ledge to brighten the place up.

I've also been doing a spot of painting! By mixing some dirty orange dust with water, I made some sticky paint and have decorated the walls with pictures of my friends. So far I've drawn the Steam-powered Rhino; Philly; Knee-high and Grip and Grapple.

Knee-high

Rhino

The nights are very chilly, and as I don't have any blankets I've stripped one of the blue trees of all its leaves, so that I can cover myself with a layer of them every night. That's where I am now, quite cosy under a pile of warm leaves with Mad Dog, staring out over the silent alien landscape. The sky is glowing with a soft light, like a great sheet of frosted glass lit by a weak bulb. It's all so weird here – I wonder how far I am away from home and if I'll ever get back? I hope something happens soon or this huge, empty planet could become a teensy bit boring.

Leaping Lizards – Close Encounters Of The Weird Kind!

I spoke too soon, I didn't mean anything like *this* to happen! I'm in a dark, damp cellar, hiding from the most ridiculous looking creatures I've ever seen! There *is* life on this planet – and right at this moment I wish there wasn't! Let me explain what happened.

After a lazy morning, Mad Dog and I set out on our usual sortie to look for fresh food and explore more of the planet. Choosing the more solid ground, we travelled for miles and my clothes were soon soaked from the moist air. I'll have to keep an eye on Mad Dog, I thought, looking at the mechanical pooch as he delved amongst some pebbles – the metal parts of his body are already showing signs of rust and if I'm not careful, he could seize up altogether.

Then, as we skirted the base of a dome-shaped hill overlooking a flat plain, I saw Mad Dog's ears prick up.

'What is it, boy?' I whispered. 'Did you hear something?'

'Waorrr,' he whined.

Then I heard it too. A noise like a ruler being flicked on the edge of a table; a springy sort of noise and, as we hid behind an orange rock, a small and very strange creature bounced onto the plain from behind a pile of boulders.

It looked like a very fat, green sausage. From the top of its metre-long body, two eyes swivelled left and right on the end of soft, snail-like horns. It had no arms or legs but propelled itself along by squashing its body until, like a coiled spring, *boing!* it let itself go, leaping forward through the air. *Boing, boing, boing!* The animal kept jumping ahead and looking frantically around.

'It's scared,' I muttered. 'It's looking for a place to hide.'

'Woof!' barked Mad Dog, his tail wagging like crazy, and I just managed to grab his collar before he darted forward.

'No, Mad Dog, stay!' I ordered. He whined and whined – the poor dog must have thought his dreams had come true – he was seeing a stick that could throw itself!

'Shh! There's something else coming,' I whispered, for now I could hear the *thump, thump, thump* of heavy feet pounding the earth.

The sausage creature panicked and stupidly boinged out into the open as six large, ungainly, fat, gormless, lolloping, lizardy-type things burst onto the plain, very close to our hiding place. They looked like crazy cartoon characters, with large, orange heads topped with purple cockscombs. They had fat, round and scaly bodies, short legs and thick tails. The creatures were as tall as me and looked rather comical – but then one opened its mouth in a slavering bellow and they didn't seem funny any more. Its cavernous crimson mouth had a set of long, poisonous-looking fangs that dripped with a mucus-like saliva. Here is a sketch of one:

The stick thing bounced away over the plain, squeaking in panic. Like a pack of hounds, the alien lizard-things heaved themselves after it. *The poor thing,* I thought, but before I could think how to help, the lizard in the lead flicked out its long tongue like a chameleon, grabbed its prey and gulped the poor sausage creature down whole!

'Ahh! Hisss, oi, oi oi,' the lizards guffawed, slapping each other on the back with webbed and clawed hands.

'Grrr!' Mad Dog growled at the back of his throat. He didn't like the look of these alien predators any more than I did.

'Shh!' I whispered. 'They'll hear you.'

But I was too late, for one of the scaly brutes bounded up the slope to where we were hiding and leered over the top of the boulder.

A-Hunting We Will Go! Tally ho!

I gasped in horror and Mad Dog backed away, barking in fear. Then I stared in amazement as, in a hissing voice, the purple-tongued lizard said:

'Ssso! What'sss all thisss? A couple of invadersss, yesss?'

'No, no; we're not invaders. I crashed onto your planet – we're marooned. My name is Charlie Small and we need your help,' I cried, trying to make this revolting reject from Toon Town understand we meant him no harm.

'Ssstranded, yes?' the lizard cooed in a liquid voice as the rest of his gang loped up, sniggering and pointing at Mad Dog and me. 'No mummy, no daddy here?'

'No, just me,' I said, wondering where he was going with this.

'Fassa, soosie soss, yeurkss?' one of the other aliens asked.

So, I thought, *English is not their natural language.* They must have learnt it from somebody though – maybe there are other humans on this planet, after all.

'Ssslan yoss, ssnnss,' the first alien replied. Then, turning to me, he said, 'Borisss isss asssking what you are.'

'I'm a human being, from planet Earth,' I explained.

'Oh, I know what you are, Charlie Sssmall,' smiled the lizard. 'It'sss only poor old Borisss. He hasn't got much of a memory sssince a revolting, dry-skinned Earthling sssky-craft 'crasssh-landed on hisss head.'

'My Gravitator landed on Boris?' I gasped. I didn't believe it. Surely I would have noticed a blobby lump like him under my feet?

'Not your ssship. Sssome other Earthlingsss a long time ago,' he hissed.

'Other Earthlings? Oh, that's brilliant news. Where are they now?' I cried.

'Oh, dear! Sssorry to disappoint you, Charlie, but we are Gerk hunterssss and have to sssurvive on what we catch, yes? We chased the invadersss and ate them with a nice glasss of ssnorasss juice. Lovely!' he said with a revolting slurp whilst rubbing his tummy. 'Now it'sss your turn, Charlie.'

'My turn for what?' I asked, suddenly very nervous again.

'To be chased and caught and eaten, of courssse!'

'No! I come in peace – I'm friendly, honest,' I cried.

'I believe you. Trouble isss, we're *not* friendly – but we'll give you a head sstart of five minutesss, yes?'

'Hold on,' I said. 'This isn't fair!'

'Four and a half minutesss. You're wasting time, Charlie.'

The Monoliths

Oh, heck! 'Come on, Mad Dog,' I yelled, and together we belted off across the open plain towards an outcrop of strange vertical rocks in the distance.

The ground was soft and springy, quickly sapping the strength in my legs, and by the time we reached the tall monoliths, the Gerk hunters had already started after us. As we ran through the undergrowth that grew between the columns of stone, we could hear the distant thump of their feet and their faint cries of 'Oi, oi, oi!'

'We haven't got long, Mad Dog,' I said. 'They can move pretty fast.'

'Woarr,' whined the pooch, his electronic eyes scanning the swift-moving monsters.

'Come on, let's try to lose ourselves amongst these rocks. It's our only hope.'

We waded through tangles of strange twisted weeds, turning this way and that between the massive smooth boulders that towered over us.

We crouched behind one of the monoliths as the Gerks came crashing through the undergrowth all around us.

'We can sssmell you, Charlie Small,' cried the lead lizard.

'We can sssmell you,' repeated the other alien reptiles.

'Sssmell,' mimicked Boris.

'Grrr,' Mad Dog gave a low growl.

'Ssh, you nit,' I whispered, clamping his muzzle shut with my hand. The Gerks were getting closer and closer.

There's no choice, we've got to get out of here, I thought. We'll have to skirt around the back of the stones, right under the Gerks' noses!

'Follow me,' I whispered to Mad Dog. 'And *keep quiet*, OK?'

Mad Dog nodded his head and I let go of his muzzle.

Slipping And Sliding

Hardly breathing, we edged past the slobbering Gerks.

'Your sssmell isss ssstrong, Charlie,' the leader called, rooting amongst the tangled undergrowth.

'Ssstink bad,' yelled Boris.

Charming, I thought, as we crawled into a high bank of blue, rubbery shrubbery. You're the one dribbling rancid snotty spit all over the floor! Then all of a sudden we emerged from the other side of the bushes and found ourselves at the edge of the biggest, deepest crater imaginable.

It was enormous; at least two miles across and one mile deep, and in the depths I could see flashes of reflected light as things moved over the bottom. What was going on down there – are they people? I wondered.

Then I heard a noise behind me. I looked to the left and right and realized I was in a terrible position. I was standing on a slab of rock that jutted out over the edge of the crater and the only escape route was back through the shrubs; at that very moment, though, the branches started to shake, and a second later my six Gerky pals were standing in front of me.

'Sssuch a ssshame! Charlie has run out of ground, yesss?' grinned the chief hunter.

I reached into my rucksack for my lasso, ready to fight.

'It'sss all over, Charlie,' said the Gerk with a smile and the gang of reptiles marched towards me. Involuntarily, I stepped back – into nothing! For a second I stood on the edge of the crater, arms windmilling like mad, then I dropped like a stone.

'Aaargh!' I cried.

'Woof, woof!' barked Mad Dog, peering down at me as I fell. Then, 'Yeeoof!' he cried as one of the Gerks booted him on the backside and he came tumbling after me.

The sides of the crater whipped past me in a blur, and I'd only just had time to get really scared when, *oof!* I landed on something with a bone-crunching thump and a splash. I started to slide down, and looking around realized I was in some sort of large, stone gutter that curved away in front of me like a gigantic flume. *That was lucky*, I thought. *I didn't notice this from up top. If I'd fallen a metre either side, I would've plummeted right to the bottom of the crater!* The chute gushed with icy water and I was swept along with it at breakneck speed.

Looking back, I saw Mad Dog, eyes wide with fear, shooting down the slide behind me.

'Stay still, Mad Dog,' I yelled above the rushing of the wind. 'We're in for a bit of a ride.'

Yeehah! What a ride it was! We flew along like bobsleighs, banking first to the left and then the right as the chute took us deeper and deeper into the crater. Soon we were down amongst a network of high monorails made of polished stone that curved all around us.

Now I could make out houses and streets, all made from the orange rock of the planet, and I realized I was travelling in the city's water supply pipe. *How strange*, I thought. I always assumed

cities on other planets would be made of shiny steel and glass. Hi-tech, computerized worlds with doors that swished open automatically, flying cars and bullet-shaped trains. But this place looked very ordinary.

There were curved satellite dishes on the roofs of the houses, but they were rusty and crudely made; there were the monorails that wound between the roofs and chimneys, but they didn't carry super-fast trains or passenger pods floating on a bed of air; only odd-looking bicycles, each with a blobby, puffing Gerk pedalling away like mad. Some of the cycling lizards spotted us, and their jaws dropped open in astonishment!

In the streets below were crowds of other Gerks, going about their business. Oh yikes! It suddenly hit me that I was shooting straight into the lion's den and had no way of stopping. Maybe these Gerks would be friendlier than the hunters, but it was a risk I couldn't take. I had to get off this slide before we ended up skidding into some sort of waterworks substation and right into the arms of a Gerk official.

'It's now or never,' I yelled to Mad Dog. 'Come on, boy!' Tucking my arms to my sides, I

rolled over the edge of the chute and dropped.
I aimed to land on the roof a few metres below
– but I missed. With a splat I fell headlong into
a tall rubbish skip, at the back of a deserted alley
between two Gerk houses.

I sank into a mess of decomposing Gerk
vegetables. Ugh! It was revolting, and I was just
trying to get to my feet when, *thump!* Mad Dog
landed on top of me and I fell into the queasy
quagmire again!

'Yowl!' Mad Dog howled.

'Quiet, you twit!' I scolded him as I wiped
some gunk from his snout. 'Do you want a
million Gerks on to us?'

Gerk Central

From under a huge, stinky vegetable leaf, I
peeped down the alley. It was very quiet, so I
carefully climbed out. The ground was rock
solid – perhaps that's why the Gerks
had chosen to build their
city down here. Mad
Dog jumped down
beside me.

I hid in a
rubbish skip!

'You stay there,' I said. 'I'm going to check this place out.'

I tiptoed to the end of the alley and looked up and down the street. The city was massive but the light was poor and the streets were lit with lanterns that threw strange, shifting pools of lime-green light onto the orange pavements. There were endless streets of cube-shaped, flat-topped dwellings; some were only two storeys high, others great towering blocks. Overhead, the bike monorails wound themselves like a tangled web, and further back, tall chimneys pumped clouds of sulphurous smoke into the air.

The road that our alley opened on to was very quiet, but where it met others at a wide intersection, it swarmed with Gerks. Some looked just the same as the hunters – dribbly, orange, fang-toothed monster cartoons; but there were many different sorts of scaly, alien reptile – long, short, fat, thin, scary, daft, purple, blue and pink! Spotted, blotched, striped and marbled; the variety of Gerks was amazing.

I ducked back into the alley. What was I to do now? We had to get out of Gerk City; if we hung around too long, we'd be sure to get

A spotted Gerk that I spotted

caught. We'd have to wait until the city became quiet, though, and all the Gerks were tucked up in bed.

All of a sudden, a square of pale, flickering light appeared in the wall of the alley behind me as a side window in one of the houses lit up. The muffled strains of familiar music drifted out and I whispered to Mad Dog to come over.

'Stand there,' I said and holding on to the sill I stepped on his back and peered into the room. I couldn't believe what I saw! The room was furnished with a table, a bench and one lumpy, carved armchair, all made from the bluish wood of the strange trees I had seen up above; sitting on the floor was a tiny young Gerk staring up at a large TV screen set into the wall – and on the TV was one of the soap operas from earth!

That's what those huge satellite dishes on the roofs must be for! I thought. The Gerks could pick up transmissions from hundreds of thousands of miles away, and that must be how the hunters had learned to speak English! As I watched, the toddler waved his arm in the air and the channel changed and showed a programme with a cast of the weirdest, most grotesque aliens you could imagine. They looked like globules of semi-liquid fat, their mouths and eyes continually shifting and moving over their spherical bodies. Crazy – for a tribe of savage, almost stone-age aliens, the Gerks had the technology to pick up channels from all over the universe!

By mistake I stepped on Mad Dog's head and he let out a moan of protest. The Gerk child turned around and for a second we stared at each other in shock. Then I ducked down below the window and started to run from the alley. But there was now a crowd of Gerks passing the entrance. I was trapped. If one of those creatures happened to glance down the alleyway, I'd be done for.

I was staring at a baby Gerk!

I went to dive back in the skip but then, in the shadows, noticed a tiny arched window at ground level that must lead into the cellar of the baby Gerk's house. *Surely that would be safer than hiding in a rubbish bin*, I thought. It wouldn't be as slimy and smelly, that was for sure!

Dropping to my knees, I pulled at the window frame and it opened with a jolt. I slid through the gap feet first. It was only just big enough and I had to squirm and wriggle before I was through and could drop into the dark basement below. With a yelp, Mad Dog jumped down into my arms. I gave him a pat and placed him on the floor, and he scuttled off, sniffing for alien rats!

It smelt musty and damp in the cellar. I took the torch from my explorer's kit and shone it around the room. It was about five metres square, and was piled high with boxes and bric-a-brac. There was a flight of dusty stairs leading up to a door. I tiptoed to the top and put my ear against it. Silence – good! I should be safe here for a while and later on I'd be able to crawl back out and get away from the city.

I've just finished writing up my journal and I suddenly feel totally exhausted. I think I'll stretch out on some of the boxes and close my eyes for a minute . . .

Gerk Hospitality

Oh, yikes! That was the wrong thing to do.

When I opened my eyes again it was pitch black. No faint light came in from the high window, and I realized I had slept for hours and it was the middle of the night. I reached for my torch, and that was when I heard the breathing!

72

'Is that you, Mad Dog?' I whispered, and then cursed myself. Mad Dog didn't breathe of course – he's a robot; he whirrs! Now I could make out the steady tick, tick, tick of the mechanical pooch as he rested in standby mode. No, it was something else breathing and it sounded like it was just behind me.

'Who's there?' I stammered. There was no reply. I was frozen with fear. Maybe one of the hunter Gerks had sniffed me out! Taking a deep breath I span round, and at the same time turned on my torch.

'Argh!' cried the baby Gerk, shielding its eyes with a webbed hand.

'Oh, sorry little fella, ' I said, directing the beam away from its face. 'I didn't mean to scare you.' I was very relieved!

The baby Gerk lowered his hands and stared at me with big, red eyes. It was kind of cute in a blubbery, wobbly, scaly sort of way.

'What's your name?' I asked. 'I'm Charlie Small. I'm marooned here. Perhaps you could tell me how to get out of this crater?'

The Gerk smiled at me, but just then Mad Dog roused himself, clicking into active mode. Seeing the weird reptile, he started barking at the top of his voice. *Woof, woof, woof!* Baby Gerk span around and, startled by the snarling mechanimal, opened its dribbling jaws and called at the top of its voice, 'Sssnark, sssnark, sslivle poosh pah!'

'Stop it, Mad Dog,' I cried. 'Ssh, baby Gerk thing, the pair of you will wake the whole house!' But they already had. There was a clump of running footsteps overhead, the door down into the cellar flew open and there stood Daddy Gerk. He didn't look friendly at all!

He had a long, bendy snout and a big mouth that opened and snapped shut like a trap door. His scaly back was covered with great, warty lumps that had clumps of hair growing from them, and his eyes seemed to glow like coals in the dim room.

'Sssloe ssslabbadan richnnar sssoop,' he bellowed, leaping down the steps in one jump.

'Ssslbadan ssssssnood,' cried the youngster.

'Run for it, Mad Dog,' I yelled and made a dash for the tiny open window, clambering across the boxes and forcing my head and shoulders through the gap. Mad Dog was right on my heels, but just as I thought I might make it, a large hand clamped itself around my ankle

and pulled me back into the cellar.

'Ssso, it'sss true isss it, yes?' the Gerk said, speaking in English and thrusting his blubbery face into mine.

'What's true?' I stammered.

'It wasss on the evening newsss,' hissed the bulbous blue Gerk, running a fat purple tongue over its lips. 'Invadersss ssseen in the sssity.'

'No, I've already told the hunters, I'm *not* an invader. I crashed on your planet by mistake. I'm stranded and need help to get back home,' I said. 'You've got to believe me, I don't mean you any harm.'

The Gerk stared at me, thinking long and hard, and then said, 'Thisss way,' and nudging me before him, directed me up the stairs. Mad Dog trotted along behind, a low continuous growl emanating from deep inside his leather body.

Midnight Feast At The Gerks!

The great Gerk directed me into a small kitchen that had a rickety table on one side and a large fireplace on the other. Set into the grate was

an old black stove with a pot gently rattling as
something simmered inside, filling the already
moist air with clouds of steam. The smell was
delicious and my tummy rumbled.

'Eat, yes?' asked the Gerk a little less sternly.

'Oh, thanks. Er, what is it?' I asked.

'Ssspleurk!' said the Gerk. 'It'sss good.'

'Mmm, ssspleurk. Sounds lovely, but I think
I'll pass, thank you.' I said.

The Gerk shrugged, but ladled some into
bowls for himself and the baby. They both
slurped the contents up hungrily and my tummy
rumbled again.

'Well, perhaps I'll have just a little,' I said, and
the Gerk dished out a bowl for me. Oh, it was
delicious, and I quickly scoffed it down.

'That was great,' I said. 'What is ssspleurk?'

'It'sss a great delicasssy,' said the Gerk. 'I'll
ssshow you.' He rummaged around
in a cupboard and brought out
a Gerk cookbook. He flicked
through the pages with his
long, webbed fingers until
he came to the right page
and then held the book
up for me to see.

'Ssspleurk,' he said.

My tummy churned and I nearly threw the whole lot back up, for on the page was a picture of the strange little sausage-shaped animal I'd seen up on the surface! Oh yikes, I'd just eaten a poor, squeaking little ssspleurk!

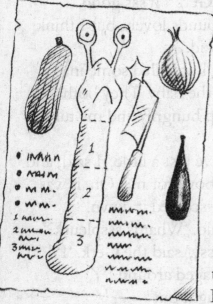

'More, yes?' asked the Gerk.

'More, no!' I cried. 'That was enough, thank you.'

'Ssso, now tell usss what you are doing here,' said Daddy Gerk.

I felt much better now I knew these Gerks were friendlier than the hunters, and I quickly told him how I'd been stranded on an out of control Gravitator and how it had plummeted onto their planet.

'Ssso, you're all alone, yes?' asked the Gerk, his eyes narrowing as he stared at me. 'There are no othersss like you?'

'No, just me I'm afraid,' I said. 'Oh, and Mad Dog here. Shush, Mad Dog.' He was sitting at my feet, still growling. 'Do you think you'll be able to help me get back to earth?' I asked our host.

'Sssure I can,' he hissed. 'But now you need a good nightsss sssleep, yes?'

'Oh, please,' I said, suddenly feeling very tired. 'But first, can you tell me how you get earth programmes on your TV?'

'TV? What's TV?' asked the Gerk.

'The big screen I saw through your window,' I explained. 'It had an old programme from earth on it.'

'Ah! The Informer,' said the Gerk. 'We get images from all over the universsse. We learn languages and keep checks on possible enemiesss; but humansss are not much of a threat. We can see they are very ssstupid!'

'Hold on,' I said, offended. 'We're not stupid.'

The big, fat Gerk shrugged his shoulders again. 'If you sssay ssso, Charlie,' he said with a hissing chuckle. 'Now, let me show you to your bed.'

I followed the Gerk and his baby up a bare flight of steps onto a landing. We went through one of a row of doors that opened on to some more steps, and then up into a small attic room where there was a low, camp-style bed . . . and nothing else. Mad Dog gave a whine of disappointment.

'Thisss OK?' asked the Gerk.

'Oh sure, it's fine,' I said, brushing at a clump of tiny green mushrooms growing on the damp duvet.

'Ssstravet sssnoe; sleep well, Charlie,' said the Gerk.

'Ssstravet sssnoe,' echoed the baby.

They closed the door and I heard their heavy footsteps go down the stairs. I waited for the click as the landing door closed before I collapsed onto the bed.

'Oh wow, Mad Dog,' I sighed. 'I'm bushed. How lucky are we to find some friendly Gerks? We could have ended up in chains, with no hope of ever getting home. Why, what's the matter, boy?' I added, for Mad Dog was standing with his ears alert, staring at the door and growling more ferociously than ever.

'OK, Mad Dog. That's enough,' I said. 'There's nothing to worry about.' But I was wrong, and Mad Dog was right to be on his guard, as I was to find out first thing in the morning . . .

The Gerk Turns

I'd fallen into a deep sleep the minute I lay down on the damp bed, and when I awoke some hours later, Mad Dog was still standing in the same place and still growling, as if his mechanism had got stuck on snarl.

Grrrr!

'I told you there's nothing to worry about,' I said, getting up and giving the automaton pooch a friendly pat. 'Come on, the Gerks might take us back to our cave today and help rebuild the Gravitator.'

I put on my rucksack and went down the short flight of stairs to the door that led on to the landing. It was locked! I turned the handle again and put my shoulder to the door, but it wouldn't budge. A tiny frisson of fear swept over me.

'Hey, what's going on? Let me out,' I cried. I still wasn't too worried. Perhaps the Gerks had locked me in for my own safety. I rattled the door and yelled again. Soon I could hear footsteps on the landing and then the rattle of a key in the door. As the door opened, I went to push my way out, but the Gerk was blocking the doorway; in his hands was a short but deadly-looking trident, and the barbed points were directed straight at me!

'I sssaid humans were ssstupid,' grinned the bloated great oaf. 'You didn't really think I would help you essscape the Planet of the Gerks, did you? You are worth far too much to me here. I am Ssslava of Ssslava's Magnificent Museum Of Oddities, and Gerkanians will pay a handsssome price to sssee a real live Earthling!'

'What are you on about?' I said, confused.

'You're going to be the latest and greatest exhibit in my museum,' hissed the revolting reptile. 'You will be the hit of the sssseason, Charlie. We will become famousss together!'

'I don't want to be famous and I will not sit in a glass case all day long so you can make oodles of cash,' I shouted, angry and scared at the same time. Mad Dog's low constant growl suddenly exploded in a cacophony of booming barks. He rushed at the Gerk, metal fangs crashing together, sparks raining down from his jaws.

The Gerk stepped back, a look of fear flashing in his eyes. Then with a snarl, he pointed the trident at the attacking pooch. Bolts of electric blue light shot from the barbs and Mad Dog crumpled in a heap at the Gerk's scaly feet. A little plume of smoke drifted out of Mad Dog's open mouth.

'What have you done, you creep?' I cried, kneeling down and resting my hand on the mechanimal's side. I know he's only a series of nuts, bolts and wiring, but he's a good and brave pal; the only pal I have on this preposterous and perilous planet.

'Ssstupid, ssstupid human,' grinned the Gerk. 'Now, downstairs and into the kitchen.' He prodded my backside with the trident as I picked up the limp body of Mad Dog and went down the stairs in front of him.

In the kitchen the baby Gerk was sitting at the

table, scoffing another bowlful of ssspleurk, and at the stove was its enormous mother.

'Sssss!' she hissed when she saw me, and taking the ladle from the pot started whacking me around the shoulders. 'Yosss, ssstrove haasss!' she hissed.

'Bansssto ssstarp, sssneep sssnasss stro,' said her husband and she stopped whacking and stepped back to stare at me with eyes that seemed to shine with fear and hatred. 'Please excuse my wife. It'sss your sssmooth, pink ssskin and hairy head, you sssee; she findsss it quite repulsive!'

The father Gerk spoke to her in their own tongue and as she listened a nasty sneer spread across her thin, rubbery lips. She left the room, only to come back a few minutes later with a smelly blanket that she handed to her husband.

'Now we are going to my museum,' said the Gerk. 'I don't want anyone sssseeing you before we get there. It will ssspoil the sssurprise, ssso you must wear thisss,' and he threw the blanket over my head. I folded it around me so I could see from a small gap and, secreting the short trident under his large, flabby arm,

All Gerks are twits!

the Gerk opened the backdoor and pushed me outside.

Still carrying the lifeless body of Mad Dog in my arms, I was hurried through the busy streets and up a long metal staircase to a terminus of the Cycle Monorail system. We waited in line until it was our turn. Gerks stared curiously at me in the blanket and asked my captor incomprehensible hissing questions, which he answered with a laugh, patting me on the head. What was he telling them?

Eventually it was our turn, and the Gerk swung a short leg over a bike and put me in a large metal basket on the front. Then we were away, whizzing over the rooftops on a thin rail that wound past chimneys and satellite dishes.

Other rails branched off in a hundred different directions and I watched through the folds of my blanket as the Gerk pressed a series of buttons on his handlebars that changed the points ahead, taking us onto the rail of his choice.

About twenty minutes later we came to a stop and I was lifted bodily out of the basket.

'No noissse now, Charlie,' said the Gerk as he led me down the steps from the monorail, along a wide street thronged with smelly, shuffling Gerks, and up a narrow side street. My mind was a whirl of confusion. What could I do? If I cried out for help I might end up in an even worse position. I decided to bide my time and wait for a chance of escape.

At the end of the street was a small, quiet square and on the decrepit building that faced us was a sign that read: *Ssslava's Hoisssisss Cramptisasius Soss*, which I guessed must mean Ssslava's Magnificent Museum of Oddities!

The Gerk unlocked the door, and once inside I pulled the blanket from my head. I was in a small, dark room but could just make out an arched box office window on our left and some swing doors ahead. The Gerk pushed them open.

'Here we are, Charlie,' he said, turning a

switch. A row of lamps that seemed to be filled with a glowing, lime-green jelly lit a large, lofty room in an eerie glow. The walls were running with moisture, the air was fetid and everywhere you looked were display cases containing the remains of the most fantastical life forms you could ever imagine.

Some of the moth-eaten exhibits

'Welcome to my magical museum,' said the Gerk proudly, leading me past the empty, staring faces of long dead exhibits. Whether they were stuffed or preserved in formaldehyde, or simply waxworks it was impossible to tell, but the poor, moth-eaten creatures made a pitiful display. The Gerk seemed oblivious to this, though.

'These creaturesss come from all over the universssse; from the far cornersss of ssspace. Some found their way here by accident, just like you. Others had the audasssity to attack usss and paid the price. You, my only *live* exsshibit, will be the sssentrepiece of my remarkable presssentation; the jewel in the crown of all thessse wondersss, Charlie,' said Ssslava.

'Well, I'm very grateful I'm sure,' I said sarcastically. 'But if you ask me, half these things look ready for the ssscrapheap.'

The Gerk looked at me malevolently. 'Think you're sssso funny, yesss?' Then, jabbing me with the trident he herded me along the row of cases and shoved me through the open glass door of the very last one and slammed it shut behind me. 'Not sssso funny now, are you, Earthling?' he hissed through gritted fangs.

'Let me out or else!' I bellowed, banging on the reinforced glass walls.

'Or else what?' came the Gerk's response, muffled by the thick pane between us.

'You'll see!' I shouted. 'Just you wait!'

'Sss, sss, sss,' smirked the Gerk in amusement and with a wave, he turned and walked away. The lamps dimmed and I was left alone in the semi-darkness, trapped in a glass prison and surrounded by dead aliens. Oh, brilliant! Can things get any worse than this?

Trapped!

Yes, they can!

I spent the rest of the day, all night, and all of today on my own in the spooky museum. Talk about boring! It's like living in a bubble. Luckily, I had been left a small pile of fruit in the corner and my drinking bottle was full of water slush. I'm so glad he hadn't left a bowl of ssspleurk for me to eat!

The Gerk returned a bit earlier to tell me he'd been busy advertising his wonderful new exhibit all over town and will reopen his museum first thing tomorrow. He's expecting huge crowds and hopes I'll put on a good show.

'Try a little bit of sssnarling and roaring, Charlie. Crowds love that sssort of thing!' he said. Well, he can keep on hoping. I'm not a performing seal, for goodnessss sakesss. (The hissing is catching!)

Now I'm alone again, although it's hard to

feel lonely with a crowd of glassy-eyed aliens staring at me from every direction. Some are like pure white balloons with small, black dots for eyes; others have eyes like huge yellow orbs as big as dinner plates. There are creatures as tall as giraffes that look like giant lobsters with nasty claws and huge horns; there are aliens labelled Sprists that look almost human, but with thin bendy arms and fluted suckers for fingers, and there are others that are little more than massive maggots, with razor-sharp fangs.

What a place to spend the night! Talk about feeling as if you're being watched. I'm finishing writing up my journal in the gloom,

Sprists looked almose human!

SPRISTS

surrounded by these beasts. I've checked my poor mechanical friend for life again, and now, with a damp blanket over my head, I'm going to try to get some sleep.

It's two hours later, and I'm still wide-awake. My brain is buzzing with too many thoughts to sleep. The reinforced glass of my cabinet is over three centimetres thick and, apart from some small air holes about two metres above my head, it's completely solid. Despite trying all my skills as a lock picker, I've been unable to open the glass door. Things are bad – I've got to figure a way out of here!

Exhibit A

The doors opened at nine o'clock the next morning, and a crowd of noisy and curious Gerks barged through the doors, pushing and shoving each other in their excitement, and made straight for my case.

They stared and giggled like children; they banged on the glass; they squashed their noses against it and made stupid faces; they did very

There are staring eyes all around me! CREEPY!

Get me out of here!

91

bad impressions of the way I walked or sat, or the expressions I made. Talk about humiliating – I will never make silly monkey noises outside the chimp cage at a zoo again!

I tried to ignore the crowds, but it was impossible. If I turned my back on them, they rattled the glass until I turned around, and if I yelled at them to shut up, they liked it even more!

When I got really fed up, I rushed at them and hammered the glass with my fists, shouting and screaming, but my adoring public just cheered like the stupid great oafs they are. Eventually, I covered myself with the blanket and sat as still as I could.

This didn't last for long. The crowds hadn't paid good money to look at a blanket, and soon I heard the door being unlocked. I looked out from the folds to see Ssslava close the door behind him. Uh-oh – he had the trident in his hands.

'I sssaid I wanted a good show, Charlie,' he said, and jabbed at me with the giant fork. Blue sparks flashed from the prongs and a bolt of electricity made me leap from the floor. 'That's better,' sneered the Gerk.

He jabbed again and I leaped away, but I wasn't quick enough and another jolt sent me sailing through the air to land with a thump against the glass. For the next few minutes Ssslava had me running around the case like a loon, desperately trying to avoid the trident's electric sting, and the audience lapped it up, cheering and stamping their big flat feet on the ground.

Eventually, Ssslava stopped taunting me and ushered the spectators out of the museum; but I'd hardly had time to get my breath back before a new crowd was shown in and the show started all over again. This went on for the rest of the day until Ssslava finally closed the doors on the last of the crowds.

'Good show,' said the greedy Gerk shaking a large sack of coins outside my display case. 'Tomorrow there will be even more Gerks wanting to sssee the wild Earthling! Here, eat thisss. You must keep your ssstrength up, yes?' Ssslava opened the door and threw in some more fruit and a bottle of slush water.

I was ravenous after my exertions and I fell on the food, shoving it in my mouth and glugging down the sweet liquid.

'Ssstravet sssnoe, Charlie,' said my Gerk guard and left me on my own in the darkening, creepy museum.

The Next Day

Big crowds; lots of knocking on the glass and silly gurning. I didn't want to be zapped by Ssslavia's trident again, so I jumped about and scratched my armpits like a monkey. I threw myself at the glass and roared and generally acted like a wild thing. The moronic crowd was delighted. More fruit for supper. (Oh boy, what I'd give for a nice juicy burger!)

And The Next

This evening something really worrying happened.

I spent the day performing for more Gerks. The crowds were bigger than ever. Then, soon after Ssslavia had shown out the last of the spectators, the swing doors crashed open and three muscle-bound Gerks marched down the corridor between the display cases. They were covered in big, armoured scales and held vicious-looking tridents with long, steel handles in their webbed hands. Ssslavia looked petrified as they started waving some papers in his face and barking orders at him in Gerkanian.

One of the Security Gerks

I couldn't understand a word, of course, but it was obvious by the way the Gerk muscle men kept pointing at me that *I* was the reason they were here. Then, with one last roar, they snatched Ssslavia's trident from his hand, turned on their heels and marched back out again. Ssslavia was left staring dejectedly at the document they had left him.

'Ha! They took your trident! Are you in trouble, Ssslavia?' I cried, delighted that he wouldn't be able to jab me with it any more.

'Bad newsss, for both of us I'm afraid, Charlie,' he said in a wavering voice. 'They were sssecurity guards for the League of Gerkanians. Only *they* are supposed to own an electric trident, so they confiscated mine, dash it.'

'And who are the League of Gerkanians when they're at home?' I asked. I wanted as little to do with those scaly hulks as possible.

'They are our ruling council. They've heard all about you and want to quessstion you. They know from watching the Informer that although ssseriously ssstupid, Earthlings are a maliciousss and dangerousss speciesss,' said Ssslavia. 'They captured a human once before who was ssspying out the land, ready for an invasion of Gerkania.

They think you must also be a ssspy.'

'I'm no spy!' I cried.

'They are coming to take you to the Inquisition Block first thing in the morning,' said the Gerk. 'It'sss not nice there. They have roomsss full of torture gadgets. You will confessss to anything once they get you in there!'

'What sort of torture gadgets?' I gulped.

'Machines that tickle your feet until you pass out from laughing,' said the Gerk.

'That doesn't sound too horrific,' I said. *Surely I can stand a bit of tickling,* I thought.

'There's a machine that drops spiders on you . . .' said the Gerk.

'No problem, I like spiders,' I interrupted him – *as long as they're not as big as the spitting Spidion,* I said to myself with a shudder.

'. . . And machines that drill a hole in the top of your head and slowly suck out your brain,' continued Ssslavia.

'Yeurk! You're kidding!' I cried. 'You've got to get me out of here, Ssslavia. You've got to hide me.'

Tickle, tickle!

(see my Journal The Underworld)

'No can do, Charlie. I'm in enough trouble for not reporting you ssstraight away,' said the Gerk. 'If you aren't here when the League Ssssecurity Guards come, it's me who'll end up having my brainsss sucked out!'

'This is dreadful!' I exclaimed.

'Yesss, it isss,' hissed the reptile. 'My plans are ruined. Ssstill, it wasss good while it lasted. I've made a tidy ssstash of cash.'

'Oh, that's all right then,' I cried. 'As long as you're OK. What about me?'

'Thingsss look very bad for you, Charlie, yes? Well, it can't be helped – see you in the morning,' said the Gerk and left me in the dark.

It's very late now, and the Security Gerks will be here in just a few hours. I've tried everything to get out of here – I've used the Megashark's tooth and my penknife but they don't even scratch the glass. I had another go at picking the lock with the bony finger I collected on the Mummy's Island but it was impossible. I tried a running karate kick against the pane and nearly broke my leg; I shouted for help at the top of my voice until I was hoarse, but it was all to no avail. I was well and truly trapped.

(see my journal The Mummy's Tomb)

In desperation, I had another go at mending Mad Dog's circuitry. *If I can only get him working,* I thought, *he might be able to chew a way out with his metal molars.* I can't seem to fix him, though. His circuits look as if they've been fried.

Now I've brought my journal up-to-date and it looks like I'm for the torture chamber in the morning! If this is the last entry in my journal, you'll know my brain has been hoovered out of the top of my head. Goodnight!

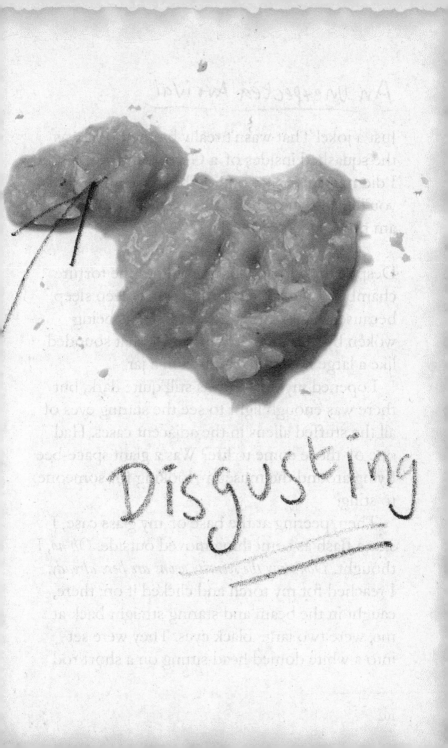

An Unexpected Arrival

Just a joke! That wasn't really brain goo (it was the squashed insides of a Gerkanian fruit!) – but I did manage to get out of the museum, and you'll never guess how it happened, or where I am now!

Despite my worries about going to the torture chamber, I must have drifted into a deep sleep, because the next thing I remember, is being woken by a strange buzzing noise that sounded like a large mosquito trapped in a jar.

I opened my eyes. It was still quite dark, but there was enough light to see the staring eyes of all the stuffed aliens in the adjacent cases. Had one of those come to life? Was a giant space-bee flying around the museum, looking for someone to sting?

Then, peering at the base of my glass case, I saw a flash as something moved outside. *Oh no*, I thought. *Don't say the security goons are here already.* I reached for my torch and clicked it on; there, caught in the beam and staring straight back at me, were two large black eyes. They were set into a white domed head sitting on a short rod

102

attached to a metal box. Underneath the smooth box were two caterpillar tracks. I was staring at a mini robot!

I was looking at a little robot

With a faint whirr, the eyes swivelled round to peer back at the glass; on the end of one of the robot's hinged, tubular arms were two metal fingers. The robot placed them against the glass; with a click his hand started to spin very fast like a drill, and the sharp fingers began to score a hole through the window. A small circle of glass dropped from the pane and hit the floor with a clink. The robot's claw-like hand closed, retracted into the metal tube of its arm, then reappeared and opened out with just one finger – a tiny, silver saw! The robot placed the blade in the hole and with a grinding noise, the saw started to oscillate and cut a thin wavy line through the glass.

I watched as the little robot cut one, two, three, four sides of a square. With a whirr it knocked the pane with its other hand and the square fell out with a thump. The robot poked its head inside my glass prison.

'Please to follow me,' it said in a metallic voice, like a crackly radio.

Without thinking to ask where it had come from and why it was helping me, I pushed my rucksack, then Mad Dog and myself through the gap and clambered out into the large room. I was free!

'Where do we go now?' I asked the robot.

'Please to follow me,' he repeated. Then, looking at the inert body of Mad Dog, the robot said, 'Oooh! *Kaput?*'

'Yes, *kaput*,' I said.

'Poor Mad Dog; I will fix later,' intoned the robot.

'You *know* Mad Dog?' I gasped.

'Of course,' said the little robot and then backed up, turned on his tracks and zoomed off down the corridor.

Escape From The Museum

I hurried after the robot between the cases of staring, spooky aliens. We raced through the foyer, and into the small ticket office.

'Slow down. Do you have a name – or serial number or something?' I asked the robot as it pushed open a door at the back of the office. It opened onto a fire escape, external stone stairs that led down to a small, dark backyard.

'POD, a Personal Operative Droid,' said the robot.

'Pleased to meet you, Pod,' I said. 'My name's Charlie.'

'Likewise, I'm sure,' responded Pod.

'So how do you know Mad Dog – and where are you taking me?' I asked, suddenly aware that this benign-looking machine could be leading me straight to the League of Gerk's torture chamber.

In response the little machine stopped at the top of the steps and opened a flap on his chest.

'Mad Dog is good friend. We were made at same time,' droned Pod as he took out this actual piece of paper.

Jakeman! I cried. 'You're another Jakeman invention – oh, brilliant, has he come to rescue me?'

'No,' said Pod.

'But . . .'

'Shush!' crackled Pod, a little antenne spinning on top of his small domed head. 'I can sense League Security Guards nearby. Now, quiet and follow me.'

I thought Pod might have trouble negotiating the stairs, but the caterpillar tracks angled down, their deep tread gripped the edges of the steps, and with a whirr from his motor he rolled to the

bottom. I crept down after him. We stood in a
deep shadow at the base of a wall, next to an
opening onto the street. Pod extended his metal
neck and looked around the corner. He glanced
to the left and right.

'All clear,' he droned and we hurried down the
dimly lit street.

'Where are we going?' I asked again.

'No talking. Gerks everywhere,' said
Pod sternly. 'This way.' His electric motor
hummed as he led me on a confusing route
through the twisting lanes of Gerk City.

As we hurried down a dim alleyway we
heard the loud slap of alien feet coming
towards us.

'In here,' whispered Pod and pushed me
into a doorway as a group of gurgling Gerks
emerged from the gloom. I held my breath as
they passed by. One of the Gerks paused and
sniffed at the air.

'Sssnoe ssslep ssslad?' asked one of the other
guards.

Oh, yikes! I thought. *The bloomin' thing has caught
a whiff of me,* but Pod raised his arm and with a
gentle hiss, squirted something into the air.

'Ssspana ssspo,' said the first Gerk, sniffing

again and they carried
on their way.

'What
did you
spray?' I
whispered,
once the reptiles
were out of earshot.

WHIFF!

'Air freshener,' said Pod. 'It always confuses
them!'

The Great Stink! ~ Pooee!

We continued ducking and diving, creeping
and sneaking through the lanes. I followed
Pod into a dark, dirty courtyard surrounded by
tumbledown houses.

'*Wooh! Wooh! Wooh!*' a deep, bellowing bark
shattered the silence and a manic, snarling
four-legged fiend rushed at us. It had a short,
powerful, spotty body and a blunt, ugly and
snarling face. With flashing eyes and a set of
horrible snapping gnashers, it launched itself at
us.

'Whoa!' cried Pod.

'Yikes!' I yelled. 'What the heck is that?'

'It's a Sssnorgler hound, a vicious guard pet,' whined Pod.

But as the muscular ball of fury sailed

The Sssnorgler hound!

through the air, it was yanked to a halt by a thick rope tied to its collar and crashed to the ground with a loud yelp. A window opened in one of the houses and a large Gerk looked out.

'Sssnee sslar sslam?' he shouted.

'Run!' whispered Pod and we pelted out of the courtyard and down a short lane before he could spot us. We came to a dead-end An arched wooden door blocked our path.

'Oh no!' whirred Pod. 'We've come the wrong way.'

I tried the door but it was locked. As I fumbled for the skeleton finger key in my rucksack, the frenzied Sssnorgler hound suddenly appeared at the end of the lane, spitting and hissing like a boiling kettle. A short, frayed length of rope hung from its collar – it had gnawed right through it! With a bellow the thing bolted down the lane towards us.

Shaking like a leaf, I clumsily pushed the skeletal finger into the lock and twiddled and twisted it until at last I felt a click. I pushed the door open, stumbled into a dark passage beyond and slammed it behind us. A split second later the door shook with a mighty crash.

As the hound butted and scrabbled at the door, I fished out the wind-up torch from my explorer's kit with trembling hands and flicked it on. We were standing in a passageway that ran between two houses.

'Quick, before it breaks through,' whispered Pod. We raced to the door at the other end of the passage. Pod opened it carefully and looked outside. 'Aha! Please to follow,' he droned and we ran out across a wide street and through some tall wooden gates on the opposite side.

We were in a deserted piazza, surrounded by shops and stalls that had closed for the night. The little robot rumbled to the centre of the square and, after scanning the ground, hooked his metal fingers into the handle of a stone manhole cover (or should that be a Gerkhole cover?). With a whirr from his motor, he lifted up one side to reveal a dark hole in the ground. *Wow!* I thought. *He's bloomin' strong for such a tiny robot.*

'In you go,' Pod whispered. A flight of steps led under the square, and I ducked inside and raced down them as fast as I could.

Pod whizzed in behind me and lowered the cover back into place. The steps were hewn out of solid rock and led us down into a large subterranean tunnel about four metres across. We stood on a raised, narrow walkway. Below us, a stream of water flowed along the bottom of the tunnel and an overwhelming stench filled the air.

'Oh yikes!' I cried, my voice echoing back from the curved walls. 'This is disgusting. Where the heck are we?'

'In the sewers!' droned Pod. 'What's the problem?'

'The smell!' I rasped, choking and coughing. 'How can you stand it?'

'I'm a robot,' said Pod. 'No sense of smell. Come on, danger is all around us.'

You're not kidding, I thought as I followed him along the walkway at the side of the channel. If you can imagine what a human sewer might smell like, let me tell you, a Gerk sewer is a thousand times worse. Phewee!

'You're lucky you're not conscious for this adventure,' I whispered to Mad Dog, who was still slumped in my arms and getting heavier by the minute. He has a very sensitive electronic nose!

Once again we were in a sort of maze, though this time underground. I followed my little metal friend down one drain after another, sometimes taking narrow wooden bridges across the yucky stream to reach a tunnel on the opposite side.

What a pong!!

'Nearly there,' intoned Pod.

'Nearly where?' I asked. In all the excitement I had completely forgotten to find out why the robot had rescued me.

'At my master's house,' said the droid.

Uh-oh, I didn't like the sound of that . . .

The Green Man And The Emerald Lady

The passage swept around in a wide curve, and on the far side Pod stopped. 'We have arrived,' he said.

I looked around. The tunnel curved away into the gloom in both directions.

'There's nothing here,' I whispered.

Pod gave a metallic sort of sigh and, with

a whirr, one of his hands disappeared into his tubular arm and reappeared as a four-pronged key. Then his arm grew longer and longer. He reached up to a crack in the rock near the top of the sewer tunnel and inserted the key. Pod turned his hand and somewhere deep in the rock I heard a click.

With a grinding noise a section of the tunnel wall began to slide forward on polished stone runners, and I stepped out of the way to avoid being pushed from the walkway into the fetid water below us.

Pod led the way behind the thick section of wall to a secret passage. The wall closed behind us, and the echoing splashes and the stench of the sewer were blocked out.

'Safe now,' crackled Pod, but I still felt nervous.

The secret passage climbed steeply until it came to a hatch above our heads. Clicking and whirring like a clockwork toy, Pod's whole body lifted from his caterpillar track feet on a pair of thin metal legs, until he could push the hatch open. He carried on growing until he'd risen through the hole. Next he telescoped first one leg up after him and placed its track on the floor above, and then brought the other one up to join him.

'Come on, slowcoach,' he called and, extending his arms back down through the hatchway, took Mad Dog from me and lifted him through the hole. Then the helpful robot reached down again and pulled me up into a dim, cave-like room. I glanced around nervously, not knowing what to expect.

Oh yikes! In a pool of light cast by a large jelly lamp were two feathery, ferny, hunched green monsters. They were crouched on the floor, studying large sheets of crumpled paper. *What the heck are they?* I wondered, starting to panic; *is this the meeting place of the League of Gerkanians?* I turned to escape back down through the hatch, but just then one of the creatures turned its peculiar-looking head towards me.

'Ah!' exclaimed the monster getting to its feet and ruffling its feathery hide. 'You must be Charlie Small we've been reading about in the Gerks' newspapers.'

As the creature hobbled towards me, I was astonished to see it wasn't a monster – it was a man! A man with wide, staring eyes, wild, unkempt hair and a tangled beard that reached down to his waist. His clothes, hair and eyebrows sprouted long, furry green fronds. It was the same stuff that was starting to grow on my own clothes.

The other mildewy figure rose and joined us. She was a woman with long, dark hair smeared

with wet algae. Her clothes were also hung with
emerald fronds of plant life that had rooted
amongst their damp seams.

The hunched green monster was a man!!

'So pleased to meet you,' said the woman, holding out her hand. 'My name is Harmonia and this is my husband Theodolite, though everyone calls him Theo. You're the first human being we've seen for over five years.'

'Welcome to our very humble abode, Charlie,' said Theo.

I shook both their hands, feeling a little less nervous now the couple appeared to be so friendly. They looked very ill, but there was something strangely familiar about the woman; something about the way she moved and spoke.

'Come and sit down,' she said. 'You look worn out.'

I was exhausted after my flight across Gerk City. She led me to a stool made of old rags bound together with rope, near the softly glowing lantern. I flopped down and stretched my aching legs.

'Here, get stuck into this,' said Theo, handing me a sandwich.

'Oh, thanks,' I said. 'Um, it's not ssspleurk is it?'

'No, don't worry,' Harmonia said with a smile. 'It's some tinned beef we've got left over from the stores on our space balloon.'

Space balloon? I thought as I bit into the delicious snack. I'm sure I've heard about a space balloon somewhere before. Then, looking around the room, I noticed a photograph standing on a crudely fashioned table. It was a picture of Harmonia with a freckle-faced, cheeky-looking toddler on her knee. As I studied the photo more closely, I gasped out loud – for I suddenly realized *who* that cheeky toddler was and *where* I'd heard about a space balloon.

The cheeky, chubby toddler

'What's the matter, Charlie?' asked Harmonia. 'There's no reason for you to be frightened here.'

'That's Philly when she was a nipper,' I gasped, pointing at the photo. 'You must be Philly's mum and dad who disappeared in their hot-air balloon five years ago!'

'You know our Philly?' exclaimed Harmonia – and promptly collapsed in a faint.

(see my journal The Mummy's Tomb)

Mr and Mrs Jakeman Junior

Theo knelt down, patting her hand and speaking to her in a soft voice. After a few seconds Harmonia came round and stared up at me through eyes brimming with tears. 'I'm sorry, Charlie, but it was such a shock to hear Philly's name mentioned by a complete stranger. We haven't seen her since she was a toddler. Is she all right?'

'Philly's fine,' I said. 'Though she misses you something chronic. She remembers seeing you off in the Jakeman Space Balloon, but nobody knows what happened to you after that.'

'What *didn't* happen!' exclaimed Theo. 'We visited undiscovered planets; we were attacked by intergalactic space wasps; we befriended a nation of giant bacteria and were just on our way home when our balloon sprang a leak.'

'We had to make an emergency landing on this planet,' continued Harmonia. 'We patched the balloon, but discovered we'd snapped the propeller's drive shaft in the crash. We tried to find a replacement, but the Gerks we asked were very hostile.'

'I'm not surprised they didn't help you,' I

said. 'They didn't help me either; I was chased by a pack of hunters and then locked up in a museum.'

'Yes, we read the reports about an Earthling being seen in the city. That's why we sent Pod to look for you and bring you here, Charlie,' said Theo.

'We were hounded by the hunters as well,' said Harmonia. 'Theo was captured and taken to the Inquisition Block. He endured despicable tortures of foot tickling and Chinese burns. They were convinced he was an enemy spy. Then, one day, a Security Gerk forgot to lock his cell and he managed to escape. Pod and I found him days later, roaming the orange wastelands in a complete daze.'

'We had already hidden our spaceship inside a deep hole in the crater fields,' continued Theo. 'So we needed a safe hiding place for ourselves. Eventually, we found this place. It must be some sort of underground bunker, built to withstand intergalactic attack. Luckily, it's very old and the Gerks seem to have forgotten all about it. We've been here ever since.'

'And you still haven't found anything to replace your drive shaft?' I asked.

'No. Steel is very rare up here. That's why the Gerks build nearly everything out of rock,' said Theo. 'Most of their metal is a crude sort of pig-iron and it's too brittle for what we need. We're looking for a long, smooth rod of steel or tungsten, but we've almost given up hope.'

'Given up hope, why?' I asked, shocked.

'Harmonia and I have become too weak to look ourselves. It's this climate, you see,' he explained, shaking the fronds that hung from his shoulders. 'It drains your energy over the years. We've been relying on Pod, but he hasn't come up with anything yet.'

All of a sudden, I had a flash of inspiration. 'How long does this drive shaft need to be?' I asked, for I'd just remembered where *I* had seen a long, smooth shiny pole and I was sure it wasn't made of pig-iron.

'About two and a half metres, why?' asked Harmonia.

'Have you ever seen a Security Gerk's trident?' I asked.

A Plan — Sort of!

'Yes, but . . . oh, of course, a trident's handle!' said Theo, thumping his head with the palm of his hand. 'How could we be so stupid! Why didn't you think of that, Pod? You're the one with the computer-sized brain.'

'Thought of it, tried it, abandoned it,' droned the robot.

'What do you mean, Pod?' asked Harmonia. 'You never mentioned a trident handle to us.'

'Wanted to surprise you,' explained Pod. 'First time I saw Security Gerks, I knew the handle of their tridents would be just the thing for drive shaft. Found out they are stored inside Inquisition Block, so went there one night when I was out collecting food scraps. Oh boy, never again.'

'Why what happened?' I asked.

'Inquisition Block is *bad* place. Heavily guarded by nastiest of Gerks. There is no way to break in, so pushed over some bins to distract guards and tried to sneak in main entrance. Nearly made it when my tracks slipped on steps and I clattered to the floor. I struggled to get up, but guards already on me. "You're going to the

Torture Chamber," they gurgled. "We'll frazzle your insides. We'll wipe your hard drive. We'll pull your arms off and sell you for scrap." My diodes were shaking with fear.'

'I'm not surprised!' said Theo.

'I went into a super-fast spin,' continued the little robot. 'Slipped from their scaly fingers and went zooming away with dribbling Gerks hot on my heels. Lost them in the lanes and hid in disgusting compost heap until morning. Feel scared just thinking about it. Inquisition Block is impregnable and I'm never going back.'

'Oh, poor Pod,' cooed Harmonia, patting his little domed head.

'You should never have attempted it, you silly, brave robot,' said Theo kindly.

'Wanted to go home,' said Pod with a little sigh.

We stood in silence, all thinking about our homes, light years away from this alien world. Were we really going to have to live in the Gerk sewers for the rest of our lives?

'*I'm* going to have a go at getting a trident,' said Theo all of a sudden.

'Don't be silly, darling,' said Harmonia. 'You're not strong enough to go creeping across the city.'

'But . . .' began Theo, when I interrupted him.

'No, your wife is right. I'll go,' I said.

'It's much too dangerous for a boy,' said Theo. 'Even one as daring as you.'

'Oh, don't worry,' I said, and even though I knew they were right and it would be an almost impossible mission, I was determined to give it a go. 'I'll need Pod to show me the way, though,' I added.

'No way, no how!' cried Pod. 'Too scared!'

'Please, Pod,' I pleaded. 'I can't find it on my own. Look how you rescued me from the museum – you're the bravest robot I've ever met.'

'Really?' said Pod, his antenna spinning with pride.

'Sure – never met a braver one,' I said, thanking my lucky stars that Mad Dog couldn't hear me.

Pod went quiet for a while, his computer brain considering all the options.

No way, no how!

'OK,' he said at last. 'I'll go with you.'

'We're still not sure a small boy should be going at all,' said Theo. Harmonia looked distraught but, after much arguing, they reluctantly agreed there was no alternative and I should go the following night. In the meantime, I was to get some rest.

Waiting For The Off

The bunker is a very spooky, damp and airless place, with high, plain walls and deep shadows in every corner. It's hard to imagine Philly's parents living down here for the last five years with no daylight. I can understand why they look so pale and poorly!

In the centre of the room, a single lantern casts a small pool of light. Here, Theo and Harmonia have stacked their few possessions: a pile of clothes for a bed; some tools; a small camping gas stove from the space balloon to cook their food; a bowl for washing, with water coming from an existing tap in the wall; a few books, pens and pencils and, most important of all, the large sheets of paper I'd seen them

studying when I arrived. These are the plans
of the balloon, covered in scribbled notes and
complicated workings-out.

The two castaways
seemed as pleased as
punch to see a fellow
human being and they are
looking after me really
well, fussing over me and
feeding me the tastiest
morsels from their store
of food pilfered from
Gerk City on night-
time forays by their
faithful Pod. I have spent
hours answering all their

Jakeman as a
young man

questions about Philly and Jakeman, and they've
shown me an album of old photos with pictures
of Jakeman as a dapper young man and Philly as
a chubby baby!

I told them of my many adventures; how
Philly had rescued me from Craik and how
we had been split up when the Gravitator
had rocketed into space. (I missed out the bit
about my peanuts jamming the altitude handle,
though!) Then, yawning madly, I went to sleep

on a bed of rags that Harmonia made up for me, close to the softly glowing lantern.

This morning I breakfasted on the green fronds that grow in great clumps on the walls, fried in rich ssspleurk butter. Then I had a look at the space balloon plans. I need to know exactly what I'm looking for – if I manage to grab a trident and escape with my brain intact, I don't want to get back and find it's a centimetre too short for the job!

I've just had a short nap and woken to a brilliant surprise; while I was sleeping, Theo and Pod managed to fix Mad Dog! His joints are a bit rusty and creaky, and his bark has become very high-pitched, which I think he finds embarrassing, but apart from that he is as good as new. I made a real fuss of him and when he saw his old friend Pod, his tail whirred in excitement. The two robots raced around the bunker together, Mad Dog barking and Pod's head spinning round and round with joy.

Now I've finished writing up this journal, it's time to go on my mission. I'll write more later.

The Inquisition Block Help!

'Oh Charlie, do take care!' said Harmonia, tears springing to her eyes as I shouldered my rucksack and made for the hatchway.

'This isn't right,' said Theo. 'I'm coming with you.' But when he tried to walk across the bunker, he stumbled, and we all knew he wasn't strong enough for a full-on mission that might involve running, jumping – and hand-to-hand combat.

'You must stay to look after Harmonia. In an hour's time, make your way to the hidden space balloon,' I said. 'If I'm successful I'll meet you there; if I'm captured, you won't be any worse off and can come back here.'

Harmonia gave me a kiss; Theo squeezed my hand and then I climbed down through the hatch with Pod and Mad Dog.

We followed Pod through the sewer as he took us along the winding tunnels. Eventually we arrived at a series of recesses in the rock wall that formed a ladder leading up to a manhole cover.

Pod did his growing trick again. He lifted the cover, checked the coast was clear, then stepped out on to the street.

'Shush, keep very quiet,' he whispered as I

clambered out after him with Mad Dog over my shoulder. We were on one side of a very wide avenue, lined with Gerkanian blue trees. Across the street I could see the back of a large, imposing building of dirty, orange breezeblocks. A wall, topped with sharpened flints, joined the back of the building at right angles and we ran over to the deep shadow where they met.

'This is the Inquisition Block,' whispered Pod.

'Can you grow tall enough to reach those windows above us?' I asked.

'No, too high,' said Pod, looking up with a whirr.

Just then we heard the slap of Gerk feet coming around the corner. We pushed ourselves back into the shadow as a Gerk sentry marched into sight, a short trident over his shoulder. Holding my breath and clamping Mad Dog's muzzle closed with one hand, I waited for the sentry to pass. I could feel the pooch's body vibrating with frustration; he would love to have sunk his teeth into the Gerk's behind, but he managed to control himself. (I've drawn a rough plan of our hiding place in the shadows.)

The sentry passed by the corner where we crouched, and carried on until he came to a

Not to scale!

INQUISITION BLOCK

GARDEN

Main entrance

Patio steps

Door

Garden wall

Our hiding place in shadows

Gerk Guards

Route of Patrolling guard

manhole

AVENUE

door in the flint-topped wall. He checked it was locked then carried on until he finally disappeared round a corner.

'We could have rushed him; taken his trident,' complained Pod and Mad Dog gave a quiet woof of agreement.

'It wasn't nearly long enough. It looked like a hand weapon and we need one as long as a spear. I know they exist, I've seen them,' I said. 'C'mon, let's try that door the Gerk just checked. It might give us a way into the building.'

We scampered over to the door. I took the finger bone from my explorer's kit and inserted it in the lock. With a couple of turns I heard a click and pushed the door. It creaked loudly open on rusty hinges, but nobody raised an alarm and with beating heart I stepped into a tidy garden of twisting shrubs and turquoise-leaved flowers.

We crept through the bushes to the back of the building and saw that there was a rear entrance into the Inquisition Block. A wide patio door led into an empty room, lit with a low light. I tried the handle, but this door was also locked, and there was no keyhole to pick. It was bolted on the inside.

'Do your stuff, Pod,' I whispered, and with a click of his hand he selected the circular drill that he'd used to free me from the museum. It span silently – but as it touched the glass, a high whine shattered the stillness of the night.

'Shush, for goodness sake!' I cried in a hoarse whisper, but the job was quickly done and a second later a small circle of glass tinkled to the floor. We waited in the dark for the shout of a guard, but again we were lucky and remained undetected. Pod extended one of his arms through the hole and silently slid back the bolts. We were in!

As we entered the empty room, I got the

shock of my life, for pasted on the wall was a poster; a poster with a crude drawing of me! It was written in Gerkanian but, with a snigger, Pod translated it for me. This is what it said:

Translated Version!

DANGEROUS EARTHLING LOOSE IN GERKANIA

Apprehend at any cost
Anyone assisting the invader will have their skull emptied by the Brain Hoover

Very hairy

No scales

Tiny eyes

Woolly body

Horrid dry pink skin

Scrawny neck

By order of The League Of Gerkanians

'Good likeness!' Pod added with a chuckle.

Into The Gerk's Den (Shush!)

Silent as shadows, we crossed the room and
entered a huge hall. In front of us were the main
entrance doors, and through their frosted glass
panels we could see the silhouettes of six Gerk
sentries standing guard outside. On our left, a
wide, curving staircase led up to the next floor.

'My master told me the Armoury is on
the first floor, next to the Torture Chamber,'
whirred Pod so, hugging the banister, we quickly
climbed to the next level. On the landing was
a set of double doors, decorated with large
diamond-shaped studs. The lintel above them
carried the following inscription:

SSPREASH SAMOVA SSSLISH SSSEBOM?

'Where all secrets become known,' translated
Pod. 'Oh dear, this must be where they keep the
brain hoover!'

Carefully I pushed down the large iron handle
and although the door was incredibly thick, it
swung smoothly and silently open. It was dark
inside and I pulled out my torch and switched
it on.

'Yikes!' I exclaimed, for the most horrific-looking machines surrounded us. Here was the foot-tickling machine, where the victim was manacled to a board whilst a wheel, fringed with feathers, was cranked round and round over the soles of their feet.

By the side of the foot-tickler was a gruesome granite desk and chair arrangement.

'What's this?' I asked Pod.

'The Crammer!' said Pod, as he read the instructions on a small plaque. 'A prisoner is locked in the chair and forced to do the most boring, tedious and mind-numbing homework imaginable, day after day after day. If they stop for just one second, they are given an electric jolt. By the third day, victims are usually ready to talk!'

'Diabolical!' I shuddered. We passed a platform where prisoners were put in stocks before an audience of taunting bullies, who threw rotten, stinking vegetables at them and called them names until they dissolved in tears. There was a manacle on top of a wooden post, where people had their arms strapped and were given Chinese burns. Next to this was the Scare-a-thon; a table to which a victim was tied, whilst above hung a glass box of the fattest spiders I've ever seen. It was a veritable chamber of horrors!

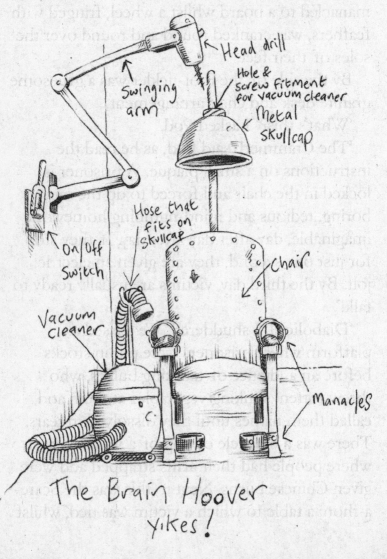

Head drill

Swinging arm

Hole & screw fitment for vacuum cleaner

Metal Skullcap

On/off Switch

Hose that fits on Skullcap

chair

Vacuum cleaner

Manacles

The Brain Hoover
yikes!

Then, on the far side of the room we came across the dreaded brain hoover, which consisted of a chair with a metal skullcap fixed to a sliding pole at the back. The cap, which would be lowered onto the prisoner's head, had a hole in the middle and above this was a drill fixed to a swinging, counterbalanced arm. By the side of the chair was a powerful vacuum cleaner with a long hose that screwed over the hole in the cap and sucked out the contents. On a shelf behind the chair was a row of glass containers, and floating in formaldehyde in each gory jar, was a brain!

'Oh yikes!' I whispered with a shudder as I read the name *Ssslavia* on one of the jars. 'They've already dealt with the museum owner, though I'm not sure anyone will notice he's had his brain removed!' I added. 'Come on, let's get out of here.' We left by a side door that led us into a wide, deserted corridor. We could hear the faint voices of Gerk guards, coming from a room at the far end of the passage.

'Ooooh! That must be the guard's common room,' said Pod, starting to get scared.

'Grrr!' Mad Dog quietly growled.

As we crept along the passage I listened at

each door then, turning the handle, pushed them open an inch or two. The first room was a dimly lit, empty canteen; the second was in darkness, but I could hear the snotty snores of sleeping Gerks and quickly closed it again! The third room I tried was a large Gerk gymnasium ... and on the far wall was the armoury – a large wooden rack filled with hundreds of gleaming tridents!

Layout of 1st floor landing in Inquisition Block

'This is it!' I whispered excitedly, shining my torch around the gloomy room.

'Rrruff!' concurred Mad Dog a little too loudly.

'Shh, you noisy mechanimal,' hissed Pod, who had been getting more nervous the closer we got to the guards.

Mad Dog looked incensed and growled even louder.

'Shut up the pair of you,' I said. 'I can't have you arguing now. The guards are just down the hall; do you want to end up in that torture chamber?'

'Sorry,' said Pod.

'Woar,' whined Mad Dog.

'That's better,' I said. 'Now come on!'

Tridents And Gerks Galore

We dashed across the gym to the rack of weapons. There were big, club-like tridents and short, sharp dagger-sized ones; tridents with three spiked balls instead of points; tridents that could be fired from longbows.

Picturing the plans of the space balloon in my

mind, I chose a long-handled electric one, the longest I could find.

'This should do the job,' I whispered to my mechanical pals, but as I pulled the weapon from the rack it got caught on something. I gave it a yank and, all of a sudden, about thirty tridents toppled from the frame and clattered noisily to the gym floor. Oh yikes! What had I done?

I turned off my torch as the doors swung open and a short, fat, long-nosed Gerk was silhouetted in the doorframe.

'Who'sss making such a racket?' hissed the Gerk. 'And if you *have* to work out at thisss time of night, why . . .' but there he stopped and sniffed the air through his snotty nose. 'Oh my, what have we here?' he said and, reaching out for a switch, turned up the lamps. 'Well, if it isssn't the Earthling ssspy.' He stepped into the gym and let the doors swing closed behind him.

I expected the Gerk to call for back-up, but he obviously wanted to catch me on his own and grab all the glory. Luckily he wasn't armed and he hugged the wall of the gym as he cautiously advanced.

I gripped the trident and gave it a few practice sweeps through the air. As I did so, blue sparks of electric charges fizzed on the ends of the prongs.

'I hope you know what you're doing with that,' sneered the Gerk. 'I wouldn't want you to give yourself a shock. *Sss, sss, sss!*'

'Don't worry about me,' I said. 'I've tackled bigger threats than you, you hissing, bubbling lump of lard!'

'Sssticksss and ssstonesss, Earthling,' chuckled the alien.

Mad Dog gave a high-pitched growl. 'Shush, boy. You'll alert the others,' I said, keeping my eyes fixed on the reptile. Then a loud noise from deep inside the building distracted me. As I glanced at the doors, praying it wasn't more guards on their way, the sneaky Gerk dashed nimbly forward, dropped to his knees and slid across the highly polished floor. He grabbed a trident from the spilt pile, and in one smooth movement got to his feet and brought the weapon swishing past my chest.

Sparks flew from his trident, scorching my shirt and sending a shock juddering through my body.

'Oof!' I cried and shot backwards, landing on my backside. The Gerk raised his weapon again.

'Ssso easssy,' he smiled. Then, 'Aaargh!' he yelled as Mad Dog sunk his metal fangs into his ankle. He dropped the trident and fell to the floor with a loud squelch, holding his injured limb.

I jumped to my feet and raising my trident in the air, brought it spearing down towards him. Two of the prongs went either side of his scrawny neck and embedded themselves in the wooden floor, pinning the reptile to the ground.

'Got you!' I cried.

'Let me go, Earthling,' croaked the Gerk.

'No way, buster,' I said. Then grabbing another long trident from the pile, I turned to my pals. 'Come on, let's go. Theo and Harmonia will be making their way to the space balloon by now.'

'Bit of a problem, Charlie,' droned Pod.

'What?' I asked.

'Those,' said Pod, pointing at the doors. Standing silently across the entrance was a line of Gerks.

'Going sssomewhere, Earthling?' hissed one of the reptiles. They were unarmed, but looked very, very annoyed.

Then they charged!

Fighting The Gerks!

As the Gerks ran towards me, I held the end of the trident and swept it back and forth. It left a tail of fizzing and popping electric light in its wake. The Gerks juddered to a halt.

'Keep back,' I said, slowly herding my adversaries into the centre of the room so I had an escape route to the doors. One of the Gerks darted forward and I swished the trident again as I backed towards the exit.

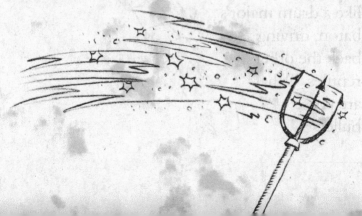

'Hisssss,' he exclaimed as a tendril of charge gave him a jolt.

But the Gerks now had access to the armoury, and they each grabbed a trident, turned and attacked together.

Yowling loudly, Mad Dog charged, gnashing his teeth and diving for the nearest reptile. *CRUNCH!* He sank his teeth into the hapless alien's hindquarters!

'Yeeow!' the beast cried.

At the same time, Pod whirred forwards on his caterpillar tracks, his arm extended in front of him and firing little hard white cubes from a barrel-shaped hand. One of the cubes hit a Gerk on the forehead and he dropped to the floor, out for the count.

'I didn't know you had any weapons!' I cried as I span my trident like a drum major's baton, driving back the other reptiles. 'What are those bullets?'

Rat-a-tat-tat

'Ice cubes,' droned Pod, firing off a further volley and stunning another Gerk. 'I started life' – *rat-a-tat-tat* – 'as an ice dispenser before Jakeman' – *rat-a-tat-tat* – 'adapted me!'

'That's handy,' I grunted. Then, *darn it!* I thought – a large, lumbering Gerk had managed to work his way around to stand between the door and me. A glance upwards, though, showed me an escape route. Hanging from the ceiling just in front of me was a row of long climbing ropes all bunched together. I ran and jumped, grabbing the end rope and hanging on one-handed, just the same as in my gorilla days. The rope rattled along a metal runner on the ceiling and I hurtled towards the snarling alien, lifting my legs high and letting out a Tarzan-like yodel. As I whooshed past the reptile's head, I kicked out at his swinging trident and sent it sailing through the air.

Then, like a circus tumbler, I let go of the rope, caught the flying trident and dropped to the floor on the far side of the surprised-looking Gerk. Now I had two fizzing electric weapons.

'Run for it!' I yelled as the rest of the Gerks advanced across the gym floor, and I bolted for

(See my Journal Gorilla City)

the door. Mad Dog released his grip from an
alien's wrist and ran after me as Pod reversed at
top speed, spraying the enemy with a shower
of rock-hard ice cubes that sent them cowering
backwards again.

I slammed the double doors behind me
and quickly slipped the spare trident through
the D-shaped handles. I was just in time, for
seconds later the door shook as the Gerks
charged, but the steel-hard trident didn't bend
and the doors wouldn't open. We were safe – for
now!

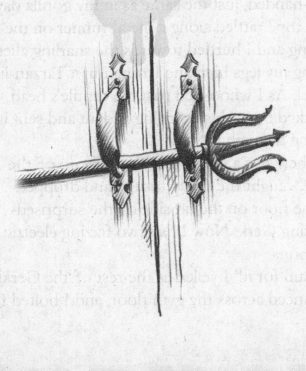

Flight From The Gerks!

We raced down the corridor as four off-duty guards sleepily emerged from a dormitory, rubbing their eyes and wondering what all the fuss was about. When they saw us they immediately gave chase. As I entered the torture chamber, I pushed down a starter handle on the wall next to the brain hoover, and the skull-drill buzzed into life, swinging crazily around on the end of its cantilevered arm.

The first two Gerks that followed were whacked on the bonce by the whipping arm, and they crumpled to the floor. The next two stepped over their prostrate buddies and charged. They were unarmed, but roared like scaly lions and displayed sets of knife-like fangs. As one rushed towards me, Mad Dog ran across his path, tripping him up whilst at full pelt.

The Gerk flew forward and landed on the platform of the tickling machine. Two large belts automatically swung over the Gerk and locked into place. Pod flicked a switch and the feathered wheel started to spin.

'No, ssstop it, *pleassse!*' squealed the Gerk, tears of laughter springing to his eyes.

Wielding my three-pronged spear, I backed the other Gerk towards the Crammer. With a jab from the trident he flopped onto the seat. I pressed a button; a hinged bar fell across his thighs and held him there. The seat swivelled round to face the desk and a speaker in the tabletop crackled into life. *'For each wrong answer you will receive one electric shock. Question one: Add fourteen and seventeen.'*

'Er...twenty, yesss?' guessed the panicking Gerk. 'No, hold on, one hundred . . . um, eleventy seven . . . erm . . . two!'

'Let's get out of here,' I cried to my friends as the Gerk desperately tried to add up the sum on his webbed fingers. Then, for good measure, I whacked the box of spiders with my trident. It shattered and the fat, hairy arachnids flew through the air and landed on the Gerk's head, just as he was writing down his answer.

'Aaargh!' he screamed.

'Too slow,' said the machine, and *Bzzz!* it gave the Gerk a jolt.

'Yeeowza!' yelled the reptile.

'*Question two,*' continued the Crammer as we raced from the chamber and down the wide staircase. Mad Dog was in the lead and when he reached the bottom he shot straight for the glass entrance doors.

'Not that way, Mad Dog,' I yelled, but it was too late. He hit the glass like a bullet. There was an almighty crash as it exploded into tiny shards and my mechanical pooch raced down the steps onto the street. Pod and I followed him, passing the astonished sentries outside.

By the time they had realized what was happening we were down the steps and had ducked into a side street. It was the middle of the night and the city was deserted.

'Follow me,' intoned Pod, leading us across streets, down alleyways and up flights of steps until we came to a monorail terminus. 'This will be the quickest way to travel,' he said. We clattered up the stairs to the empty platform. I put Mad Dog and Pod into the basket of the first bike and leaped onto the saddle. As I pushed down on the wooden pedals, we saw a swarm of sentries rushing towards the terminus steps below. They were all armed. I pedalled faster and soon we were whizzing along the stone rail, above the rooftops.

Although the crude bike was made from a mixture of stone, wood and pig-iron, it was remarkably speedy. Pod pressed the buttons on the handlebars, changing the points ahead and selecting our route. Soon a line of bellowing aliens on bikes was following us along the rail, and lights started to go on in surrounding houses. Sleepy Gerks stuck their heads out and yelled at us to keep the noise down. Then, seeing it was the Earthling spy, they rushed from their houses and joined in the fun. Oh yikes, I was being chased by a city's worth of space freaks!

I puffed and pedalled my way up a steep incline until we came to a terminus high above the city at the edge of the crater. Pod was immediately off, rattling across the platform to a tunnel in the crater wall, and we ran down the tunnel after him. We could hear the Gerk cyclists in the distance – they weren't far behind. The floor sloped steeply upwards and I was soon panting for breath as my shoes slipped and skidded on the gravelly ground. Then we emerged from a cave mouth on to the surface of the planet. The sky was lightening with the dawn and the scene was bathed in a pale, lemon glow.

'This way; not far now,' said Pod and led us along hard, rocky ridges avoiding the surrounding, squashy ground. By the time the Gerks emerged from the cave we had increased our lead over them. It was a good job too, for now there were hundreds of the drooling dolts and we heard their shouts echoing in the clear morning air.

The Balloon

Soon we were in an area dotted with craters, some no bigger than wells, others a hundred metres across. We wove a path between them, Pod confidently leading the way. Then all of a sudden he stopped in his tracks.

'What's the matter?' I asked.

'I've forgotten where the crater is,' he said. 'The crater where we hid the balloon!'

'What?' I cried.

'It's around here somewhere,' bleeped the robot.

'Woarrr!' sighed Mad Dog as I scanned the landscape. There were loads of craters big enough to hide the space balloon and it would take hours to check them all.

A noise from behind made me spin around. I gasped. Oh, yikes! I could feel the thump of Gerk feet shaking the ground. I could hear their jeering calls. 'We can sssmell you, Earthling ssspy! We can *sssee* you!'

'Think, Pod, think!' I pleaded.

'It's not easy, you know,' he said, his voice a high-pitched whine. 'They all look the same.'

The mob of Gerks was now teaming across the crater field. Some stopped and, taking longbows from their shoulders, placed thin, arrow tridents in them and aimed into the sky.

'That's it. We're done for!' I cried. Then, to my astonishment, with a noise like a roaring wind, a great yellow dome started to bulge up

The ground started to bulge!

from one of the craters over to our left.

'What the heck's that?' I said. 'The ground is starting to bulge.' The dome grew bigger and bigger. 'Look out, the planet's going to explode!'

'Calm down, Charlie,' droned Pod. 'It's the balloon. We've found it!'

As the dome grew even bigger, I could see a balloon emerging from a crater. Then a thwacking noise filled the air as the Gerk archers loosed their arrows. They arced across the sky and zipped towards the balloon, their sharp, three-pronged heads glinting in the morning light. I held my breath. If one of those tridents found its

mark, our escape plans would be scuppered –
but with a hundred thuds, the tridents hit the
ground and I breathed out. The missiles had
fallen short. The archers, though, were already
reloading.

By now the balloon was floating above the
level of the ground and I could see a silver
cigar-shaped capsule hanging underneath. As I
watched, a door opened in its side and there was
Theo, frantically waving and beckoning.

'RUN!' I yelled, and we pelted away towards
the craft. A mass of Gerks gave chase. They got
closer and closer – I could feel their breath on
my neck. There was the jab of a trident on my
backside; a webbed hand tried to grab me as a
pool of Gerk dribble landed on my shoulder.
Oh, cripes!

All of a sudden Mad Dog, who had darted
away like an express train, turned on his heels
and raced back, barking his funny high-pitched
yelps and snapping his jaws; he leaped amongst
the crowd of aliens, biting and butting them
with his bullet head. The Gerks panicked,
running in every direction, screaming and
gurgling and hitting out at the auto-dog. He
charged the archers just as they fired their

second round, sending the tridents zooming hopelessly off-course.

Theo held the capsule hanging at ground level and as I ran towards him, he rocked it back and forth, trying to make the balloon drift nearer the crater's edge. It was still about three metres from the lip as, running at full pelt, I leaped out over the deep hollow. Clinging on to the precious trident, I

Theo held the capsule hanging at ground level

landed with my top half through the capsule door and my legs dangling over the dizzying drop to the bottom of the crater below. Theo grabbed me by the collar and hauled me in.

Panting, I turned to look for my friends. As I did, Pod's metal fingers clamped themselves to the lip of the floor. He had extended his arms to their full extent and was now hauling himself aboard. Further back, Mad Dog was racing towards us, an angry mob of Gerks close behind. They raised their tridents above their heads and threw them like spears.

'Dodge and weave,' I yelled and Mad Dog started to turn this way and that, confusing the throwers and avoiding the deadly barbs as they twanged into the ground all about him. The balloon shifted and started to float further from the edge.

'What's going on?' I cried. 'We've got to wait for Mad Dog!'

'I can't control it any better, Charlie,' said Theo, turning a valve-wheel a few fractions of a millimetre. 'Without the propeller it's at the mercy of the winds.'

Mad Dog was tearing straight towards the edge of the crater, barking and yelping. It was now or never. A second longer and we would be out of his reach.

'Jump!' I screamed at the top of my voice.

Mad Dog jumped and a hundred tridents followed his flight. As his feet landed on the metal floor of the cabin and he skidded across to crash into the far wall, the tridents clattered harmlessly against the outside of the capsule and dropped into the crater below.

Theo slammed the door shut and quickly turned the valve to pump more hot air into the balloon. The balloon bulged above us and we whooshed upwards through the orange morning sky.

'Well done, Mad Dog, you're a hero!' I cried, giving his ripped and tatty leather body a big hug. 'And well done, Pod, for leading us to safety.'

'Sorry for interrupting, Charlie,' said Theo. 'We'll be leaving the atmosphere soon and I have to fit the new drive shaft, or we'll be careering across space with no control over our direction.'

I rushed over to help – I'd been in that situation before, and I didn't want to go through it again!

Back To Earth :Yipee!-

We measured the trident and then sawed away
the three prongs. Then we bolted a large,
folding propeller to one end of the trident's
long handle. Theo passed this into a tube and
fed it along, through the prop housing and out
of the capsule. Then he gave the rod a swift
turn; outside, the prop fanned open like a flower
and, with a click the blades locked into place.
The other end of the rod was inserted into the
craft's motor and secured. Next, using a handful
of the gooey Gerk spit that had dripped on my
shoulder, I greased the axle so that it turned
freely.

'All done, dear,' said Theo.

Harmonia pressed the START button on the
capsule's console and the engine puttered into
life. The new drive shaft span happily around.
Harmonia pressed down on the throttle; the
propeller span even faster. She turned the
wheel this way and that and the balloon reacted
perfectly. It worked – we had done it. Yahoo!

'We're going home, we're going home,'
chanted the couple, holding hands and
cavorting around the cabin like two children

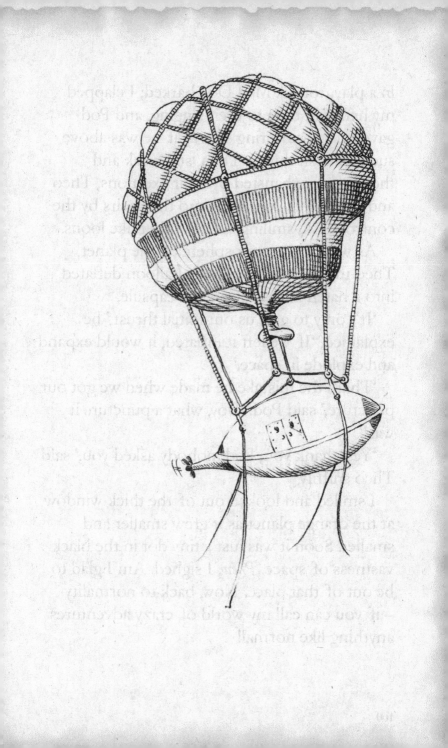

in a playground. Mad Dog barked; I clapped my hands in time to their singing, and Pod gave a long, suffering sigh as if he was above such childish things. Then, still weak and thoroughly exhausted by their exertions, Theo and Harmonia collapsed into the chairs by the control desk, smiling at each other like loons.

As we left the atmosphere of the planet, Theo turned a valve and the balloon deflated into a hatch in the top of the capsule.

'It's only to give us our initial thrust,' he explained. 'If we left it inflated, it would expand and explode in space.'

'That's the mistake he made when we got our puncture,' said Pod. 'Boy, what a puncture it was!'

'Yes, thank you, Pod, nobody asked you,' said Theo sniffily.

I smiled and looked out of the thick window at the orange planet as it grew smaller and smaller. Soon it was just a tiny dot in the black vastness of space. *Phew*, I sighed. Am I glad to be out of that place. Now, back to normality — if you can call my world of crazy adventures anything like normal!

I am curled up in a rather uncomfortable hammock in one of the two cabins aboard the space balloon. I am trying to write up my journal, but the hammock is swinging wildly to and fro as we rocket across space towards earth.

Hopefully, I will soon be back at Jakeman's factory and I can finally use his Archway to Anywhere to get back home to Mum and Dad. I'm going to finish now; I'm tired out after my adventures with the Gerks. Mad Dog is curled up beneath my hammock and I can hear Pod still busy in the galley, tidying up after the ship's long period in storage, and getting our breakfast ready for tomorrow morning. I'm sure, now I'm in the safe hands of Philly's mum and dad, that nothing can go wrong. I'll write more, later.

Space Balloon To Control, Come In Control!

Oh why oh why don't I keep my big mouth closed? Everything has gone wrong. I just don't believe it!

At first, things went without a hitch. Rattling and juddering, we entered the earth's atmosphere. Then, *BAM!* We emerged into the bright sunshine of a summer's day, falling through a blue sky towards the earth. With a mighty hiss, the balloon bulged from the hatchway above our heads and quickly swelled to its full size. The capsule stopped dropping and, checking our coordinates on a beeping green screen, Harmonia turned the controls and directed us towards Jakeman's factory.

After breakfast I was wandering around the cabin, studying all the knobs and dials, when I noticed an old-fashioned telephone receiver. I picked it up and heard a dial tone.

'What's this for?' I asked Theo.

'Oh, that's how we used to keep in touch with Dad, back at his factory. It hasn't worked since we left the earth's atmosphere,' he said.

'Well, it seems to be working now we're back in the earth's atmosphere,' I said. 'Listen.'

Harmonia snatched the receiver from me and held it to her ear.

'He's right,' she gasped. 'There's a dial tone. Theo, we can speak to our darling Philly!'

'Brilliant!' Theo and I cried together.

'Oh dear,' said Harmonia, tears springing to her eyes. 'I don't know if we should. What if the shock's too much for her? What if she doesn't know who I am?'

'Don't worry,' I said. 'She'll know who you are. She talks about you all the time. What if I speak to her first; break it to her gently?'

Harmonia looked nervously at her husband. 'Should we?' she asked.

'Oh yes. I think the shock would be much worse if we just turned up at the factory without any warning at all,' he said.

I dialled the number that Theo handed me on a scrap of paper and I heard the phone start to ring. I waited and waited, Harmonia wringing her hands beside me, but no one answered. 'Maybe they've gone to the shops,' I suggested, about to replace the receiver, but just then I heard a tinny voice on the line.

'Hello. Jakeman's World Of Inventions. Hello? Sorry, Gramps and I were just welding a tailfin to a rescue rocket. How can I help you?' asked Philly.

'Philly? It's me, Charlie. I'm on my way back to your factory,' I said.

'Oh Charlie, thank goodness,' she cried. 'We've just been making a machine to come and look for you. Where are you? Where have you been? How long are you going to be?'

'We should be with you tomorrow,' I chuckled.

'We? Are you with somebody?' she asked.

'Yes, Phil. Now look, are you sitting down, because you're in for a bit of a shock,' I explained.

'Oh, I don't like the sound of that. What's wrong, Charlie?' Philly asked.

'Oh, nothing's wrong. It's a nice shock. I've got two people here who really want to talk to you. Two people you haven't seen for a long, long time,' I said.

'People I haven't seen for a long, long time?' she said, a bit confused. 'But the only people I really, really want to see are . . . oh, Charlie, you don't mean? Oh my goodness. Oh, jeepers!'

'I'll hand you over,' I said and passed the phone to Harmonia.

Well, for the next two hours Harmonia and then Theo, and then Harmonia again, were chatting non-stop on the phone to their long-lost daughter. There were tears of happiness; there were shrieks of joy; they laughed and cried and then laughed again. While they chatted on and on, I did my best to steer the balloon in the direction I thought we should be heading. It made me feel a bit sad, listening to them talk to their daughter. I wished I could have a good chat to my mum and dad. I'll have to try my mobile again, as soon as I get to Jakeman's factory.

Eventually, after a hundred goodbyes and see-you-soons, Theo and Harmonia put the phone down. They were glowing with happiness, and Harmonia came over and gave me a great sloppy kiss on the cheek.

'Thank you, Charlie,' she said, and I blushed as red as a beetroot!

How It All Went Wrong oh no!

We flew through the rest of the day, all through the night and into the following dawn – and that's when it happened. We were flying over a huge jungle and, sometime during the night, we must have descended too low. Suddenly, there came a terrible grinding noise and we drifted to a stand-still.

'What the heck?' said Theo. He opened an inspection panel at the back of the capsule and looked out. 'Oh cripes! There's a tangle of creepers caught in the propeller.'

I peered past him and saw a nest of foliage wrapped around the prop. It would have to be removed if we were to stand any chance of steering a route back to the factory.

'Charlie, my boy,' said Theo, blushing with embarrassment. He looked a lot more human since he'd had a shower, changed his clothes and shaved off his beard, but he was still very weak. 'The propeller needs to be freed, but we can't land in that thick forest. Could you clamber out and give it a go?'

The balloon had drifted higher into the air and the forest was far below us, but I knew it would be dangerous to descend too close to the treetops again. *Looks like I'm going to have to do some sky-walking*, I thought.

'OK,' I said, with a gulp.

'Are you sure, Charlie?'

'Yeah, sure I'm sure,' I lied.

'We could tie a rope around you, so if you do slip you won't fall too far,' beamed Theo.

'Yes, please!' I said. 'I've got just the thing, too,' and I unrolled the lasso from my explorer's kit.

Yikes!

Within a couple of minutes I was stepping out through the main door onto a small metal ledge that ran around the middle of the capsule. The ledge was slippery and a strong wind was blowing.

'Are you sure the rope is tied firmly?' I cried above the buffeting gale as I edged along the ledge towards the propeller stem, my hands trying to find some grip on the smooth metal hull of the craft.

'Don't worry, Charlie,' yelled Theo. 'It's as solid as a rock.'

I reached the point where the smooth body jutted out to form the housing of the prop shaft. It was about two metres long, and at the other end was the tangled-up prop. With arms outstretched like a tightrope walker, I edged my way towards the end. Then, sitting down,

I gripped the casing with my legs and leaned forward to free the knot of vegetation.

Way below me, the green, unbroken canopy of the jungle stretched to the horizon in every direction. *Don't look down*, I told myself as I started to feel dizzy. *Concentrate!*

I grabbed a handful of leaves and woody stems and yanked. It came away from the prop easily, but I could see a long vine wrapped tight around the drive shaft that was causing all the trouble.

Reaching into my rucksack, I took out the Megashark's tooth and started to saw at the stems. They were tough, but the giant tooth was sharp and the strands started to ping apart.

Then, all of a sudden I was through – the freed propeller span into life; the capsule jolted forwards and I dropped from my precarious perch.

Thank goodness for the safety rope, I thought – but as I dropped, my lasso fell into the path of the spinning prop blades and was sliced in two!

'Help!' I yelled, falling like a stone.

'Oh Charlie,' I heard Harmonia cry from the capsule doorway. The trees rushed up to meet me. I closed my eyes, waiting to crash through the upper branches of the jungle. Then:

Bump!

I hit something, but it didn't feel like the hard, scratchy branches of a tree. I opened my eyes and gasped – I had landed on something cold and scaly, and seemed to be flying through the air! I was on the back of a massive, low-flying . . . what was it – a dragon, or maybe some kind of leathery Jurassic monster!

The gigantic creature flew as fast as an aeroplane (and it was about the same size too), and when I looked over my shoulder, Hermione and Theo's balloon was already a pinprick in the distance. With each flap of its enormous

serrated wings, the creature covered miles of blurred forest below and I grabbed hold of its protruding, bony shoulder blades to prevent myself from falling off. Behind, a long sinuous tail snaked in the air, and in front an equally long neck led to a bony, sharp head.

Throwing back its pointy snout, the creature let out an ear-piercing call. I don't think it even felt me drop onto its back. The thing was so big, and its brain had to be so small in that little skull, you could probably drop a piano on its back and it wouldn't feel a thing! I clung on for dear life.

We left the green carpet of jungle behind and crossed a landscape of rolling hills; we passed over a high region of lonely lakes and finally, as the sun began to set, we came to a vast plateau of wind-blasted scrubland. Then, as the flying monster suddenly tilted back and began to climb higher, I was taken by surprise and rolled across its back, along its narrow tail and fell from the sky . . . into a deep bed of frosty moss.

A Monstrous Vision 👀

An icy wind set my teeth shivering like a pair
of castanets. I clambered from the bank of
mossy plants and looked around me, my
breath forming clouds in the chilly air. The
harsh undulating landscape of rock and scrub
looked bleak and unwelcoming. *Double darn it!*
I thought. I'd been so close to getting back to
the factory to be with Philly and Jakeman again;
so close to being cannoned back to my own
world, and here I was at the start of yet another
perilous adventure.

I looked up at the darkening sky. It was filled
with pulsing colours; purples and ice-blues;
pinks and magentas that swirled across the
heavens like oil in water. It was beautiful, and
I stood staring at it, hypnotized by the shifting
spectrum. I smiled to myself; there's no way I'd
experience wonderful sights like that back at
home. Perhaps having another adventure won't
be such a bad thing after all!

Then the cold hit me again, and I knew I had
to keep moving if I didn't want to be frozen
to the spot. Taking my tatty old coat from my
rucksack, I wrapped it around me and jogged

off across the barren tundra. Soon it grew dark – and that's when I first heard the snuffling of an animal close by. I looked around, but couldn't see a thing in the gloom.

Quickening my pace I started to run, my feet ringing on the cold rocky ground, and sure enough the footsteps quickened behind me and the snuffling turned to a low growl. Oh yikes! *What now?* I thought. My heart started to beat faster and a sweat broke out on my forehead, despite the cold. I ran for all I was worth, weaving this way and that through the dark, trying to confuse my pursuer.

Then all of a sudden, the ground dropped away from under me and I went tumbling down a steep bank, spinning like a top, and crashed into a towering wall of rock. Scrambling to my feet I ran full-pelt along the base of the tall cliff until I spotted the entrance to a deep gash in the rock. I dived inside, lay down on the floor and tried to listen above the noise of my own gasping breath.

There was nothing at first, and then I heard the growling beast again. Another noise joined it and the growl rose to a roar. A blood-curdling howl filled the night air followed by a

yikes!

tremendous snarling and crashing. It sounded as though a mighty battle was taking place out there in the dark.

A scream echoed in the air; then I heard the disgusting sound of teeth ripping through flesh and the slurping, burping noises of a predator gorging itself on its kill. A shiver ran through my body. Eventually, though, the unknown beast had had its fill. I heard its footsteps disappear into the distance and everything became deadly quiet again.

It's cold and dark and the night is full of danger, so I'm going to stay in this deep crevice for the night and try to get some sleep. It's not the coziest place I've ever stayed in – at the back of my hideout is a great, thick sheet of ice where a tumbling waterfall has frozen solid and a cloud of frosty air swirls over its surface. Still, I'm not going to moan about it – I am having a series of the most unbelievable adventures ever recorded!

I've just finished writing up my journal and am trying to get comfy on the hard floor. I'm looking forward to the morning, when I'll find out exactly what sort of place I've landed up in, and what sort of animals I'd heard fighting. I'm . . . hello, what's that?

I've just noticed a faint shadow *inside* the frozen waterfall, but a crust of frost is obscuring it. If I brush the frost layer away, I might see what's trapped inside. There we . . . *Oh yikes!* Right in front of me, imprisoned in the solid ice wall is the figure of a monstrous Tyrannosaurus Rex! The petrified beast is perfectly preserved in its icy coffin and is looming over me with its jaws frozen in an open snarl, displaying teeth as long as cucumbers! Was it one of its living relatives that had tracked me over the tundra? I thought these bloomin' things were meant to be extinct.

Shush! Now I can hear a noise coming from outside my cave again – a sniffing of huge nostrils. A tremendous roar has erupted just outside; a massive blunt, snorting snout is trying to push its way into the rocky crevice, blowing clouds of warm steam into the air around me. Its jaws are opening. *Please go away, please go away, please . . . Heeeelp!*

PUBLISHER'S NOTE

This is where Charlie's journal ends, and it looks like the eight-year-old adventurer is in *real* peril! We want to know what happens to our young hero in this new land of prehistoric predators, so please, please, *please* keep your eyes peeled for a brand new Charlie Small journal. If you find one, be sure to send it to us without delay!

www.charliesmall.co.uk

PREDATOR RATING 50

GERKS

Revolting, reptilian aliens that live in Gerkania City. They are devious, dangerous and not to be trusted. If they capture you, they will take you to the dreaded brain-hoover!

WILD ANIMAL COLLECTORS CARDS

There wasn't a card about gerks in my collectors card pack, so I made one up myself!

A sketch of one of the Gerks that came to see me in the museum

You can colour it in if you want - I didn't have time!

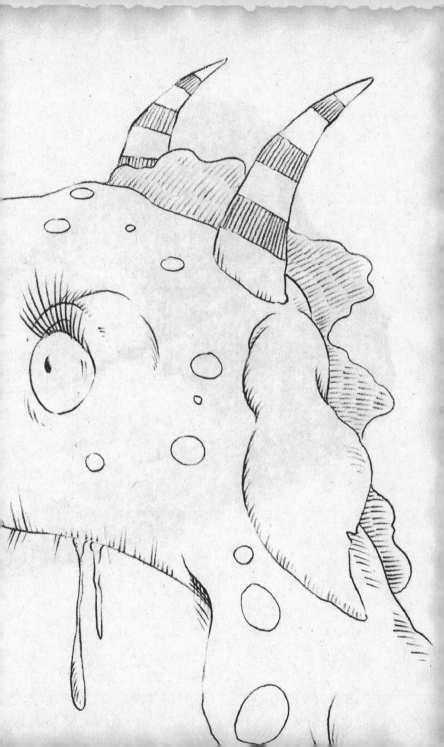

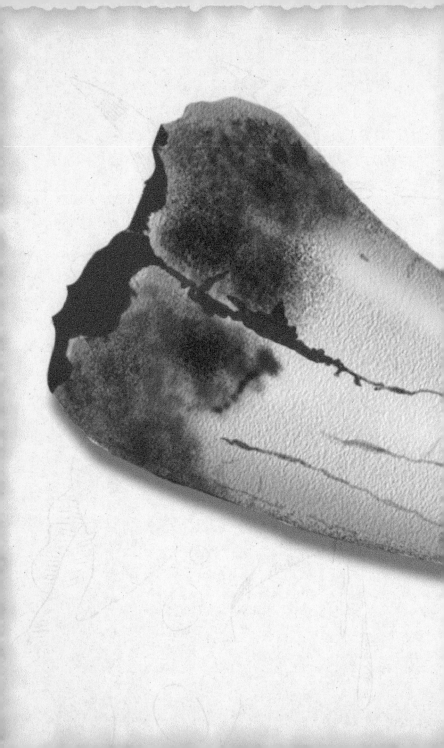

Oh yikes! I've just found this old dino-tooth on the ground. Imagine the size of the monster that this gnasher came from!

Some Space Jokes groan!

Where do astronauts
leave their spaceships?
— At parking meteors!

What do you call
a space magician?
— A flying sorcerer!

What do you call an
alien with three eyes?
— An aliiien!

What is an
alien's normal
eyesight?
— 20, 20, 20!

What are aliens
favourite sweets?
— Martian-mallows!

Why didn't the
astronaut get burnt
when he visited
the sun?
— He went at night!

What is
a spaceman's favourite
game? — Astronauts and
Crosses!

How does an
alien count up
to 25? — On
its fingers!

Charlie Small's tips
for Space Travel

1) Always plan your trip in advance – try to avoid accidental space travel

2) Make sure your space craft has got an MOT!

3) Pack a stun gun!

4) Always make sure you will be able to get home

5) Always be prepared for alien treachery!

6) Never call an alien a fang-toothed, slimy blubber-ball – it just might understand you!

7) Go with a friend – a strong, brave, karate expert, if possible

Happy Exploring!

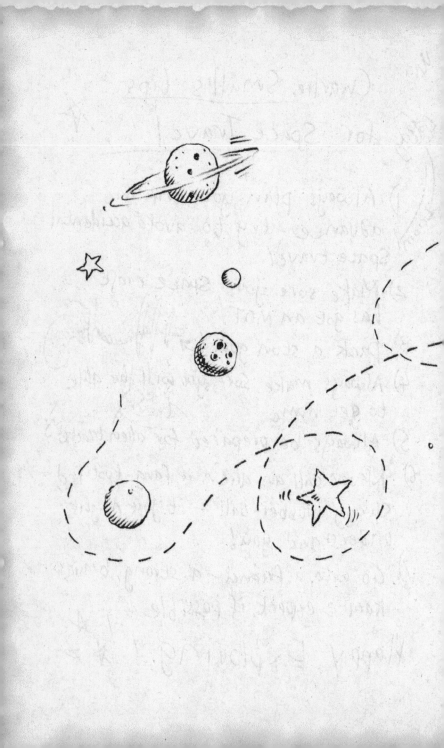

Draw your
own gerk here!